LEO AND THE GAME SQUAD

A MIDDLE GRADE SCIENCE AND HEALTH ADVENTURE

DR. SPARK

GENAK PUBLISHING

ISBN: 978-1-970490-00-8

Illustrations by GENAK Publishing

Published by GENAK Publishing

This is a work of fiction. Names, characters, places, and incidents are either the product of the author's imagination or used fictitiously.

Disclaimer: This book is for educational and entertainment purposes only and should not be considered medical advice. Always consult a healthcare professional for personal medical guidance.

CONTENTS

For my son,
whose curiosity, laughter, and love of games sparked this story, and for his Sunday school friends, fellow middle school adventurers learning to balance controllers, books, and healthy food.

May you always find joy in play, wisdom in learning, and strength in healthy choices.
You are the real heroes—discovering that life itself is the greatest adventure.
Game on, heroes!

"When we balance fan activities like gaming, reading, sports, and eating healthy, we get tremendous power in life --The Power-Up"—Dr. Spark

"Balance is the greatest power-up."
— Flo, Game Guide

Review reminder

Your honest review helps other readers discover this message—and reminds bookstores, libraries, and discussion groups that balance; healthy choices, gaming, and adventures all matter in a child's overall growth. Gift a child or friend with this book today.

Email: DrSparkAuthor@gmail.com

Where to Review:

Amazon

Barnes & Noble

Goodreads

Apple Books / Google Play Books

Thank you in advance for your honest reviews.

READERS

Welcome to the Squad!

This isn't just a story—it's a mission. You're about to jump inside Leo's body to battle sugar sludge and beat the brain fog.

As you read, watch for clues from Flo and Agent T. After each chapter, check the **Power-Up Questions** to boost your own stats. Would you make the same choices as Leo?

You are the boss of your own body. Are you ready to defeat the junk food monsters and level up?

Tell your parent or teacher to get a **Teachers Version** for discussions, questions, and fun activities.

Game on!

LEVEL 1:
Into The Game

LEVEL 1
INTO THE GAME

Leo's mom set down a tray of lemonade and watched the three kids sprawled across the living room. Jamal had claimed the beanbag, his sixth-grade soccer jersey still grass-stained from practice. Nia, the youngest at fifth grade, sat cross-legged on the carpet, her glasses slipping as she sorted through a pile of game controllers. Leo, the oldest in seventh grade, stretched across the couch like he owned it.

Three military families. One block. Their parents served together, and so did they.

Hours earlier, Jamal's mom and dad had pulled up in their uniforms, duffel bags packed tight. Nia's parents arrived minutes later. Hugs were quick but fierce. "Be good for Mrs. Carter," they said. "We'll call when we can." Then the cars rolled out, bound for the base and a peace mission in Gaza. Leo's dad had already been deployed for two months. Now it was just Leo's mom holding down the fort for all four kids.

Leo's little brother Marcus, only five, was already asleep upstairs. He didn't understand why Dad's video calls came at strange hours, or why Mom looked tired even when she smiled. Leo did. And tonight, he didn't want to think about it.

The house felt quieter than usual. Nobody talked about it. They just played.

Leo's thumbs hammered his controller. Pixel flames exploded on the TV as the Mega Boss towered above. He dodged a split second too late. His hero blinked out, fragments flickering across the screen.

GAME OVER.

Leo slumped against the couch. His hands tingled, eyes burning with gritty exhaustion.

"You zoned out, man! The boss telegraphed for like five whole seconds." Jamal nudged him.

Though he'd seen the move coming. His brain noticed, but his fingers dragged behind.

"What's happening to my fingers?" Leo asked.

"Rematch?" Nia asked, pushing her glasses up.

Leo shook his head. "Something's weird. Not the game. Me."

Jamal yanked the controller over. "Lemme show you how it's done."

From the kitchen, Mom called, bright and insistent. "Dinner! Chicken, broccoli, rice. It's hot!"

They all groaned.

"Broccoli again. Those trees want to take over my plate," Leo griped.

Jamal flopped backwards. "My tongue's on strike."

Leo pushed up, legs creaky, his head stuffed with cotton. In the kitchen, Mom had laid out a home-cooked meal, but the real lure was the spread of chips and sodas from their gaming marathon. Leo crunched handfuls of chips, chasing the tang with sharp soda bubbles until he coughed.

"Leo." Mom's look meant business. "Dinner means at the table, with us."

"I'm eating," Leo protested, even while crumbs flew.

But it wasn't real eating. Just an itch he couldn't scratch. A quick buzz that faded to emptiness. He kept reaching for more.

Nia and Jamal did what they were supposed to. Forks in hand, they started eating dinner.

Leo hovered by the counter, snacking until Mom insisted he sit down. He poked at his food and snuck chips behind his plate.

By nine, his stomach twisted. By ten, he couldn't focus. By eleven, he could barely keep his eyes open.

Nia yawned, nearly losing her glasses. "Do we have to finish the final level tonight?"

"One last shot," Leo managed, half-hearted.

Jamal's head drooped, eyes shutting.

The couch pulled them in. TV light washed their faces in tired blue. The game music looped on, but no one played. They faded, half-awake.

Leo whispered, "Just one more..." but sleep caught him.

The screen faded. A new soundtrack started. A low, thunderous rushing.

A strange weightlessness washed over Leo. The couch turned into a wave. The room stretched, grew translucent. Lights blurred. The sounds changed. Wet, swooshing, loud, like being underwater. Then the floor slipped away.

The Drop

Leo plummeted sideways through a glowing tunnel. Giant red discs zipped past his head, nearly knocking the air from his lungs.

"WHAT IS HAPPENING?" Jamal's voice echoed.

Leo clawed for something solid. All he caught was heavy, warm air with a faint metallic tang.

In the shadows of the bloodstream, a sharp-eyed figure waited. Agent T, a legendary memory T-Cell. His badge glinted. His aura was crisp with suspicion as he scanned the newcomers. He'd seen all sorts of invaders, but this squad was different. His gaze lingered on Nia's eyes, on the strange reflective things they called "glasses," mirroring the red flow. "Odd camouflage," he muttered into his wrist communicator. "Possible viral agents. Initiate watch protocol."

A green blur zoomed toward Leo. He shouted. It hovered. Someone, or something, with neon green skin and sneakers that flashed with every step.

She grinned. "Flo. Your tour guide. Welcome inside your body. Try not to wreck the place."

Leo gaped. "I... This can't be real."

Agent T slipped closer, invisible to the kids but visible to resident immune guards. He fired off orders: keep lookout, gather intel, report anything strange. His files on Nia grew by the second. "Glasses. Unknown function. Alert level: high." He flagged Jamal for nervous energy, Leo for unusual host activity, and Flo for potential inside job. His presence stiffened the road's defenders, who froze with a hint of unease. When Agent T called in backup, everyone listened.

Flo flipped and stuck the landing on a glowing walkway. "Real enough. See those red discs? That's your bloodstream. That's Hemo." She waved at a disk with a cartoon face carrying a bubble.

"Special O$_2$ delivery!" it called, zipping away.

Flo nodded. "He's reliable if you feed him."

Nia stared in shock. "We're really inside Leo?"

Flo shrugged. "Short on water, too. See that river? That's hydration. You'll need it." She hurried down the tunnel.

Jamal panted beside them. "So... how long till Leo's brain checks out?"

Flo peered down the rushing current. "Ten minutes, maybe. Those snacks didn't help."

Nia tripped over her words. "Wait, what?"

They rounded a corner and skidded to a halt.

The Blockage

Five greasy trucks had crashed, blocking the main road. Gobs of sludge clogged everything. Red blood cells stacked up, oxygen bubbles sputtered, sirens screeched.

A huge jeep barreled up. An immune cell leaned out, yelling into a megaphone. "CODE RED: ALL UNITS TO THE BRAIN GATE!" Chaos exploded as immune cells raced to clear the wreck, only tangling things more.

Flo's eyes darted. "Not good."

Leo's voice came out thin. "Are... we stuck?"

Flo grabbed Leo's arm. "We've got to clear that, or your brain's going nowhere. We'll be here a while."

Jamal gulped. "He'll sleep forever?"

Flo steadied herself. "Not forever, but you'll all feel like zombies."

Part of the highway flickered and dimmed.

Leo swayed.

Flo clapped. "Leo! With me."

"I'm here." He forced himself upright.

Flo signaled. Bristly helpers rolled in with glowing mops.

"That's heavy," one squeaked.

"Don't let it win," Flo said.

She turned to the kids. "You three, grab mops. Corners are yours."

Leo eyed the sludge and remembered the bag of chips and soda. He attacked the mess with his mop. The handle hummed. The gunk vanished.

Nia stepped forward, ready with her mop. Agent T narrowed his eyes from behind a traffic cone of platelets. "Monitor the girl in glasses," he signaled. The immune cells slowed, watching her every move. "If she tries anything, intervene." The message rippled across the crowd. For every glop of greasy sludge the kids attacked, Agent T noted the results. If cleaning was a trick, he'd see through it soon.

"It works!" Nia whooped, jumping in.

Jamal jabbed at a stubborn glob. "No more weird snacks for me. Maybe."

Mac the immune guard watched, approving. "Good teamwork."

Gradually, the jam loosened. Blood cells moved forward. Vitamin trucks squeezed past.

Hemo dashed by. "Nice job, Captain!"

Leo's arms ached, but he kept going. Lights flickered back to green. The flow opened. The stream poured through. Hemo spun a quick lap.

Flo steadied Leo. "Teamwork did it. You cleared the brain highway."

Jamal wiped his brow. "Next time, chips stay out."

Flo winked. "It's about balance. Your body helps, even after wild rides."

The flow eased. Blood cells cheered. Flo celebrated. Agent T didn't clap. Instead, he logged the squad's teamwork, marking suspicions and softening just a little. "Results positive, but investigation ongoing," he reported to head-quarters. His eye still tracked Nia, but a sliver of doubt crept in. Could these "agents" be allies after all?

Mac rolled up. "You three might be the best helpers we've had."

Leo felt sharper. Wide awake. The fog was gone.

Flo said softly, "Your body handles tough jobs every day. Even small changes help."

Leo nodded. The attack, the snacks, the strange journey. They clicked into place.

"So... what's next?" he asked.

Flo's sneakers sparked. "Level two. Bigger challenges. More ways to help your team."

A sign flashed: LEVEL 2: THE BLOODSTREAM SUPERHIGHWAY

Arrows pointed ahead.

"You ready?" Flo asked, bouncing.

Nia and Jamal nodded, eyes bright with curiosity.

Leo felt a thrill. "Let's go."

Together, they stepped into the unknown.

QUESTIONS

<u>Level 1 – Into The Game</u>

1.   What do you think the grease jam stands for? What kinds of foods might cause it?

2.   Why doesn't Agent T trust the new squad at first?

3.   What makes Flo a good guide?

4.   How do you think having parents deployed changes how Leo, Jamal, and Nia spend time together?

5.   How could Leo help Marcus feel less worried about their dad being away?

6.   Why do you think the kids played video games instead of talking about their parents leaving?

O₂
O₂
O₂
SLOW CARBS
FAST SUGAR
O₂

LEVEL 2

THE BLOODSTREAM SUPERHIGHWAY

The tunnel opened into a massive chamber. Noise everywhere. Movement everywhere. Light bouncing off a thousand surfaces at once.

As the squad approached the bustling intersection of the Bloodstream Superhighway, a silent observer hunched above—Agent T, memory T-Cell, famous among the body's defenders. He scribbled notes as the newcomers moved, his eyes narrowed on Nia, whose reflective glasses flashed with every passing signal light. "Unusual group dynamic," he recorded quietly. "Priority status: high. Recommend surveillance." The presence of outsiders had stirred anxiety among patrol cells who glanced at Agent T for orders.

Leo stepped onto a platform overlooking the bloodstream. Red blood cells zoomed past in rivers, so close he could feel the rush of air. One swerved near him, and he saw the oxygen bubble on its back, glowing like a tiny sun.

"O_2 DELIVERY! Coming through!" the red cell hummed.

"Whoa," Jamal breathed.

"Yeah." Nia's voice was barely a whisper. "Whoa."

The Bloodstream Superhighway

Hemo swerved between two slower vehicles, balancing his oxygen bubble like a pro skateboard trick, and disappeared around a bend.

"Show-off," Flo muttered, but she was smiling.

Leo couldn't stop staring. The highway wasn't just crowded. It was organized chaos. Red blood cells stayed in the fast lanes. Bigger trucks rumbled in the center. Little repair vehicles darted along the edges, patching potholes in the tunnel walls.

And overhead, a golden river curved through the air, glittering like something out of a fantasy movie.

"What is that?" Leo pointed.

"Hydration line." Flo hopped onto the railing. "Water highway. Keeps everything flowing smooth."

She tapped a gauge mounted on the wall. The needle sat just below a green zone marked OPTIMAL.

"Uh-oh."

Leo's stomach twisted. "What's 'uh-oh'?"

"You're running low." Flo glanced at him. "When's the last time you drank actual water?"

Leo's face went hot. "Lunch? Maybe breakfast?"

"I KNOW."

Jamal snorted. "You literally had a can in your hand when we..."

"I SAID I KNOW."

A convoy of food trucks rumbled past, painted with bright logos. Bananas, yogurt cups, slices of bread. They smelled weirdly good, like a farmer's market crossed with a kitchen.

"Potassium, probiotics, fiber," Jamal read off the sides. "Dude, it's like your body ordered groceries."

"Basically." Flo jumped down, landing with a spark. "Electrolytes keep your nerves firing and your muscles moving. Like spark plugs."

"What happens if you don't have them?" Nia asked.

"Cramps. Brain fog. Your heart gets confused." Flo shrugged. "Not great."

Jamal made a face. "My heart can get confused?"

"Super confused. It's dramatic."

A siren wailed.

Three white jeeps with flashing blue lights swerved into view, cutting through traffic like they owned the place.

Mac leaned out the window, helmet crooked. "IMMUNE PATROL! Everybody stay calm!"

He wasn't calm. Nobody else was calm, either.

The jeeps screeched to a stop in the middle of the highway. Mac hopped out, looked around like he was searching for trouble, then spotted a piece of floating debris.

He lunged. His mouth opened way wider than it should've. He swallowed the debris whole. Then he burped.

"Streets: cleaned," Mac announced proudly.

Nia gagged. "I did not need to see that."

"You're welcome!" Mac beamed. Then his eyes locked on something behind them, and his smile vanished. "Oh no. Oh NO."

Leo spun around.

A greasy truck swerved hard, clipped a vitamin cruiser, and tipped sideways. Sludge exploded across three lanes. The smell hit Leo like a slap. Burnt oil, old fryer grease, and something sour that made his eyes water.

Mac's siren blared. "ALL UNITS…"

"WAIT!" Leo shouted.

Mac paused, megaphone halfway to his mouth.

Leo grabbed a mop from the fiber squad. "We've got this."

He plunged it into the sludge. The mop lit up, slurping the grease away in seconds. Nia and Jamal followed. Within minutes, the lane cleared.

Mac lowered his megaphone slowly. "Well. That was efficient."

Flo's smirk came back. "They're learning."

A red blood cell squeezed through, oxygen bubble glowing. The driver waved. Leo waved back.

He was helping. Actually helping.

"Come on." Flo started walking. "Tour's not over."

They followed her past glowing intersections where signs blinked: BRAIN. MUSCLES. ORGANS. Arrows lit up and dimmed as traffic shifted between routes.

"Wait," Jamal said. "The blood just... picks where to go?"

"Your body picks." Flo pointed at the BRAIN route, where three lanes were wide open. "Taking a test? Brain gets priority. Running a race? Muscles get priority."

"What if you're sitting on the couch all day?" Leo asked.

"Then nothing gets priority." Flo's voice was flat. "Everything runs on low power. Like playing a game on a dying battery."

Leo winced.

A pale blue van cruised past, steady and calm. Its side was stamped with SLOW SUGAR.

"Oatmeal, beans, fruit," Flo said. "Steady energy. Your mitochondria love it."

"Your mito-what-now?" Jamal squinted.

"Mitochondria. Power plants in your cells." Nia adjusted her glasses, looking smug. "We learned that in science."

"Nerd," Jamal muttered.

"Smart," Nia corrected.

A red van blasted past, swerving wildly. FAST SUGAR was spray-painted on the side in lightning bolts.

"Candy, soda, energy drinks," Flo said. "Great for five minutes. Crash city after."

The van zoomed toward the BRAIN gate. The lights flashed super bright, then faded until they were barely glowing. The van coughed and stopped, smoke puffing from the engine.

"Lag spike," Jamal muttered.

"Exactly," Flo said. "Your brain just crashed."

They crossed a bridge where pipes hissed and gurgled. A calm voice crackled from a speaker.

"Kidney filters here. Requesting water. Drowning in soda. Please. We're begging you."

The pipes groaned like they were in actual pain.

"Your kidneys are complaining," Nia said.

"They do that," Flo muttered.

A shiny ship slid by, leaving a sparkly rainbow trail behind it. It had a fish painted on the side and smelled faintly like the ocean.

"Omega-3," Flo said. "From fish and nuts. Keeps the walls smooth."

"My grandma's obsessed with salmon," Jamal said.

"Your grandma's a genius," Flo corrected.

They rounded a corner.

And froze.

Ahead, a sugar van had crashed into a control tower. Sparks flew. Traffic lights blinked randomly. Red, green, yellow, red, green. No pattern. Drivers were confused, honking, crashing into each other.

Agent T sprang into action, barking commands at immune units to cordon off the scene and report to him directly. Behind the scenes, he intercepted Nia, blurting a volley of serious questions. "Purpose of visit? Function of eyewear? Who sent you? State your cellular classification." The checkpoint grew tense as other immune cells gathered, whispering their doubts about the newcomers. Even Flo's reassurances held little sway while Agent T scanned for the slightest misstep.

"Oh no," Flo breathed.

"What?" Leo's heart kicked into high gear. "What now?"

"The traffic control system." Flo pointed at the flickering lights. "It's malfunctioning. If we don't fix it, your brain's gonna get scrambled signals."

"Scrambled how?" Nia's voice cracked.

"Think brain fog. But worse."

An alarm blared. The tower sparked again. Bigger this time.

"We need to shut it down and reboot it," Flo said. "Manually."

"How?!" Jamal shouted.

Flo looked at Leo.

"You're gonna have to climb the tower and flip the reset switch."

Leo's stomach dropped. "Me?"

"Your body. Your tower." Flo's voice was steady. "You can do this."

Leo looked up. The tower stretched three stories high, covered in sparking wires and flickering panels. A ladder led up the side, but half the rungs were missing.

His hands were shaking.

As Leo struggled to climb the tower and Jamal rallied the team, Agent T intercepted worried messages from nearby defense cells. He cautioned the entire squad, but especially

Nia, "Any suspicious movements will result in immediate detainment. We have protocols." His caution created a ripple of hesitation among neighboring cells. Their trust in Agent T was ironclad, born from his past victories against major invaders. The sense of trial weighed heavy as the mission pressed on.

But Nia grabbed one hand. Jamal grabbed the other.

"We got you," Nia said.

"Squad up," Jamal added.

Leo took a breath.

Then he started climbing.

The rungs were slippery. His palms were sweating. Every time he looked down, the highway blurred into a river of light that made his stomach flip.

Don't look down. Just climb.

Halfway up, a wire sparked near his hand. He yelped, jerked back.

His foot slipped.

For one horrible second, he was falling.

"LEO!" Nia screamed.

He caught himself on the next rung, heart hammering, gasping.

"I'M OKAY!"

"KEEP GOING!" Flo shouted from below.

He climbed faster. Didn't think. Just moved.

Finally, he reached the top.

A panel glowed red: SYSTEM MALFUNCTION. Below it, a big red switch labeled RESET.

Leo grabbed it.

Pulled.

The tower went dark.

For one horrible second, everything stopped. The lights, the sirens, the hum of the highway.

Then... BOOM.

The lights blazed back to life. The traffic signals blinked once, then turned green. All of them. In perfect sync.

Below, the drivers cheered. Horns honked in celebration. Red blood cells surged forward, oxygen bubbles shining.

Leo laughed. Loud and breathless and a little hysterical.

"I DID IT!"

"GET DOWN HERE!" Flo yelled, but she was laughing.

Leo climbed down. Faster this time. He dropped the last few feet, and Nia and Jamal tackled him in a hug.

"That," Jamal said, "was the coolest thing I've ever seen."

"Coolest thing you've ever done," Nia corrected.

Leo couldn't stop smiling. His chest felt like it might explode.

Flo's sneakers sparked as she walked over. "Nice work, captain. You just leveled up."

"Yeah?" Leo was still catching his breath.

"Yeah." She pointed down the tunnel.

After Leo rebooted the tower and the signals returned to normal, Agent T surveyed the cheering crowd. His features softened for the briefest moment, but his suspicion had not faded. He added a final note to headquarters:

"Squad's effectiveness acknowledged, but unexplained advantages remain. Watch list still active, especially for subject N." Yet beneath the surface, the first cracks of curiosity replaced some of his former doubt.

Ahead, a massive gateway glowed with flashing light. A sign above it read: BRAIN CONTROL CENTER.

But the lights weren't steady. They flickered. Fast. Frantic. Like a video game glitching.

"What's wrong with it?" Leo's stomach sank.

Flo's smile faded. "That's what we're about to find out."

A rumble shook the tunnel. The lights flickered faster.

And then...

Everything went dark. Again.

Flo grabbed Leo's wrist. "RUN!"

They ran.

Behind them, the gateway's lights flared back to life. Blood red.

An alarm screamed through the tunnel: "WARNING. BRAIN OVERLOAD. SHUTDOWN IMMINENT."

"What does that mean?!" Jamal yelled.

Flo didn't answer.

She just ran faster

QUESTIONS

Level 2 – Bloodstream Superhighway

1. Why is the bloodstream like a superhighway?

2. Have you ever had a sugar crash? What did it feel like?

3. Why does your body need water for healthy blood flow?

LEVEL 3: BRAIN CONTROL CENTER

LEVEL 3
THE BRAIN CONTROL CENTER

The gateway burst open. Leo, Jamal, and Nia tumbled onto a metal platform, skin prickling with static, like they'd sprinted across a carpet in socks. For a second, Leo just lay there, heart banging so hard he could barely breathe.

"What just happened?!" He scrambled to his feet.

Flo skidded in beside them, sneakers sparking as she landed. "Brain overload. Your system almost crashed again."

"Almost?" Jamal's voice squeaked.

"We're in the command center now." Flo jerked her thumb ahead. "If the system tanks while we're here, we're stuck."

"Stuck how?" Nia whispered.

Flo's face was serious. "Stuck like Leo-doesn't-wake-up stuck."

Nobody said a word.

Before the gateway burst open, deep within the fiber of the control center, Agent T positioned himself near a cluster of communication nodes. His sharp gaze flicked between the squad and the pulsing neurons. "Unknown outsiders advancing," he relayed through his communicator. "Initiate observation at maximum alert. Eyes on the girl with mirror eyes," he added with special urgency as Nia followed the others onto the metal platform. The security team tightened its ring, their respect for T's orders clear in every cautious glance.

Leo swallowed. "Then let's not let that happen."

Flo nodded and started down the platform. The metal stretched out into... well, not a room, but something huge, wild, and strange.

It was a galaxy of lights.

Billions of sparks whizzed in patterns, neurons trading signals, weaving messages way faster than any computer.

Threads connected them in shapes that looked like constellations.

Zap. A line fired.
Zap. Three more snapped back.
Zap, zap, zap.

It was a conversation. Leo could almost hear it: Think. Remember. Move.

"Whoa," Jamal whispered.

Nia's glasses caught the glow. "This is... everything?"

Flo paced along a glowing rail. "Every thought, feeling, memory, move you make. All here. All now."

In the center, a knot of lights flickered out of sync. Stuttering, sputtering, too bright and fizzing. Like a light show gone wrong.

"What's up with those?" Leo asked.

Flo's smile faded. "Sugar crash. Your brain's spotlight is glitching."

Leo blinked. "Spotlight?"

Flo tapped her temple. "Attention. Sugar cranks it up super bright, but not smarter. Just flashy. Then poof, it tanks."

They watched the flickering cluster dim, blink, and vanish.

Jamal winced. "Just like last week math test, big breakfast, then fog."

Flo shrugged. "Yep. Spotlight fizzles, brain goes blank. Come on, meet the team."

A tiny packet dashed across Leo's nose and thunked into a glowing mailbox.

"Neurotransmitters," Flo said. "Brain mail. They spread messages. Feel this, remember that, move here."

Packets streaked by, each shining a different color.

A bright yellow one hopped past, leaving a trail of sparkles.

"Dopamine," Flo smirked. "Your 'play again!' code. Win a game, laugh at a joke, eat something yummy, dopamine shouts 'MORE!'"

Jamal fist-bumped the air. "I'm all about dopamine."

Everyone laughed. Flo pointed at a blue packet drifting slowly.

"Serotonin. The chill one. Keeps your mood steady, stops you from losing it over every little thing."

A purple packet stomped past, blowing a whistle.

"Party pooper GABA," Flo explained. "Tells the wild neurons to settle down and take a seat."

A gray packet floated by, snoring.

"Adenosine. Sleep ref. The longer you're awake, the more it piles up and knocks you out."

Nia pushed up her glasses. "So my brain's like a team with coaches yelling plays?"

"Pretty much. Secret signal trading every second."

As the squad explored the galaxy of brain signals, Agent T tailed them along a catwalk high above. He jotted notes in his casebook, tracking each puzzling behavior. The others puzzled him, but it was Nia's quick thinking and constant analysis that set off extra warnings. Whenever her glasses reflected a new pattern, he leaned in, searching for hidden messages. A few patrol cells around the perimeter exchanged anxious whispers. Under Agent T's watch, nothing was getting through unchecked.

They moved deeper into the command galaxy. The lights dimmed. Some threads drooped. The air weighed heavier.

Flo stopped. Her voice dropped low. "You need to see this."

Down a side hallway: the walls were scorched, neurons sputtering or burnt out, leaving dark gaps.

"This," Flo said quietly, "is what street drugs do."

Leo froze. "Like medicine?"

Flo shook her head. "Not what doctors give. Stuff you get from dealers, cocaine, meth. Pills kids sell at parties, things they hype up as life-changing."

Jamal's voice was barely there. "Does it actually feel amazing?"

Flo snapped her fingers.

When Flo led them past the burnt-out neurons, Agent T blocked an access door. "State your intent in this sector," he demanded, making sure every cortex guard could hear. "My records show no prior clearance for your group. Especially not for you," he said, nodding at Nia. The tension was electric. Still, as the group witnessed the dangers of the system, Agent T lowered his pad just slightly, taking in their honest reactions.

The hallway exploded in horrible, blazing light. Dopamine packets hurled everywhere, bouncing frantically. For one wild moment, it was like a winning screen at an arcade.

But then: Pop. Pop. Pop.

The lights burned out. Dopamine shriveled and crashed. The whole place went cold and black.

Leo shivered. "That's it?"

Flo's sneakers barely sparked. "Drugs flood the dopamine system, trick your brain into thinking it's the best thing ever. But the circuits fry. After that, nothing feels good, school, friends, games, food. Except the drug. And some-times, nothing feels good, period."

Nia looked at the burnt threads. "Can it heal?"

Flo nodded slowly. "Sometimes. Takes years. And some, just never come back."

A shadow flickered at the end of the corridor. Too many arms, too many eyes, smile way too big. It clawed at the neurons, grabbing at packets until they burst.

Flo jumped up, blasting a shower of green sparks. The shadow yowled and melted into smoke.

Flo turned back to Leo, Jamal, and Nia. "That shadow's not real. It's a warning. One you remember if anyone ever offers you 'power-ups' in real life."

Jamal frowned. "Just... say no?"

"Say no, walk away, or tell a grown-up you trust. No short-cuts."

Nia clenched her fists. "Okay."

Leo nodded.

Jamal snorted. "Not downloading that expansion pack, ever."

Flo motioned them out. "Let's leave the shadows. Next stop's more fixable."

They turned into a gray room, walls pale and dim. Serotonin drifted slow. Even dopamine was barely moving.

Leo rubbed his eyes. "Why does it feel... heavy?"

Flo said softly, "Not enough sleep, good food, movement, sunshine. That's what low fuel looks like. This is what depression can feel like, too."

Nia thought about long nights of homework. Jamal remembered the days after his grandpa got sick. Leo recalled bored, zombie mornings.

"Can you fix it?" Leo asked.

Flo nodded. "Most times, yeah. Sleep, food, movement, sunlight, talking it out, asking for help. Doctors can help too. That's not weakness."

The room brightened, just a little.

Flo clapped. "Enough heavy. Let's find some curiosity."

They entered a new chamber. Mysteries floated everywhere, puzzles glowing, mazes humming, riddles spinning in the air.

Flo spread her arms. "Curiosity Cluster. Your brain's playground."

Leo's eyes widened. "It's like a side quest."

Nia jumped at a spinning puzzle and missed. "Ugh! How does this work?"

Leo watched carefully. The pieces formed a pattern. "Slow and steady, squad. Nia, snag the left piece when it lines up. Jamal, the right. I'll go for the middle."

Together, they clicked the fragments into a star. Blue light rippled across the room. Warmth tickled their skin.

Jamal laughed. "Better than candy!"

"Yep," Flo nodded. "And no crash."

A spiky gremlin tumbled through, tugging neuron wires into a knot.

Flo fired a spark. The gremlin screeched and let go. "Stress gremlin. Handy in emergencies, but a menace when it's always around."

It bounced away, grumbling.

Flo tapped two shining towers puffing out light, with dashboards blinking wild signals.

"That's hypothalamus and pituitary: air traffic control for your whole body. They pick who gets fuel, who gets rest, who gets alert on 'hard mode.'"

A red van labeled FAST SUGAR zoomed through, smacked into a neuron, fizzled, and died.

Jamal raised an eyebrow. "Lag spike, huh?"

"Exactly." Flo pointed at a switch. "Nia, flip the slow-carb lever."

Nia did. Oats and fruit flowed into the neurons. Steady light returned.

"That's how you keep your brain happy," Flo said. "Not a fireworks show, just a solid shine."

A rumble shook the floor.

Leo spun around. "Now what?"

Flo's eyes went huge. "Boss gremlin. This one loves chaos."

The ground split open. The biggest gremlin yet stomped out. Built of worry blocks, sugar bars, tangled wires, sleepless scribbles, it roared. It swiped at the memory belts, sending boxes of SHORT-TERM and LONG-TERM flying.

During the final confrontation with the boss gremlin, Agent T stood with a team of sentinel cells. He raised his hand, signaling the cells to stand by but not to interfere yet. "Hold your response. If they are saboteurs, the chaos will expose them. If not..." His voice trailed off, eyes locked on Nia's every move as she took action to help the group. Only when the squad succeeded did he tap out a reluctant message: "Squad neutralized threat effectively. Continue monitoring. Possible allies, but remain on alert for subject N."

Nia braced her feet. Jamal looked for something to throw. Leo grabbed a glowing rope made of oats and apples and tossed it, snagging the gremlin's arm.

Jamal heaved a water sphere onto its head. Mist fizzed off its shoulders.

Nia slammed the slow-carb switch. The neurons glowed steady. Flo fired green sparks in time, keeping the rhythm strong.

The gremlin shrank. Its voice faded. Then, poof, with a last whine, it melted into a drain and vanished.

Lights steadied. Memory boxes rolled back into place. The kids cheered. Leo felt his head clear, like spring cleaning after a storm.

Flo helped Leo up. "You balanced the level."

Jamal wiped his brow. "That was intense."

Nia smiled, tired but happy. "Fuel, rest, curiosity, all the puzzle pieces."

Leo gazed at the galaxy of his brain, still a few flickers, but shining bright enough for hope.

"What's next?" he asked.

Flo pointed down a corridor, glowing purple like twilight after sunset.

A sign blinked overhead: SLEEP SANCTUM: THE SAVE POINT.

"Time to meet the repair crew," Flo said.

The squad looked at each other. Nervous, proud, ready.

Together, they headed forward.

QUESTIONS

<u>Level 3 – Brain Control Center</u>

1.   What decisions does your brain make without you noticing?

2.   What do the stress gremlins stand for? What are healthy ways to handle stress?

3.   Why is it important to know how substances can affect the brain?

4.   How is feeling sad different from depression?

LEVEL 4:
THE SLEEP SANCTUM
MEMORY
MEMORY
DREAM
MEMORY
DREAM
DREAM
DREAM
DREAM
MEMORY
DREAM
HIPPOCAMPUS ARCHIVES
HIPPOCAMPUS ARCHIVES
MEMORY
DREAM

LEVEL 4

THE SLEEP SANCTUM

The corridor leading out of the brain felt different. Not bright. Not chaotic. Just soft. The light shifted from harsh white to something gentler, like late afternoon fading into evening. The air smelled like rain on warm pavement. Tiny moths drifted past, wings dusted with silver.

Leo's shoulders relaxed. He didn't know how tight they'd been until now.

"Welcome to the Sleep Sanctum," Flo whispered. Her sneakers barely glowed, just a soft green shimmer. "This is where the real magic happens."

Jamal yawned. "I thought we were done with boss fights."

From the edge of the corridor, Agent T showed up. A faint shadow of him casting across the soft moths. With narrowed eyes he studied the Sleep Sanctum entrance. "Squad entering critical rest sector," he reported. "Subject N appears... calm. Monitoring for deception." His tone less sharp, replaced by something closer to curiosity. Still, his hand remained near his alert beacon. "I am ready to summon backup if these guys make a wrong move."

The Sleep Sanctum: The Save Point

"Different kind of fight." Flo pushed open a door carved with stars. "This one's about letting go."

They stepped through and stopped.

The chamber was massive. A dome stretched overhead, deep blue like the sky right before stars appear. Below, conveyor belts looped around a central tower, carrying glowing boxes with scribbled labels:

New Vocabulary. Coach's Instructions. Locker Combination. Joke from Lunch. Mom's Birthday.

Little figures in navy uniforms guided the boxes toward archways carved with words: *Hippocampus Archives. Cortex Library. Motor Memory Vault.*

"What are those guys?" Nia asked.

"Sleep crew," Flo said. "They sort your day. Decide what to keep, what to practice, what to file away."

One of the figures noticed them and saluted. His whistle glinted like a tiny star.

Agent T hung back near a memory archway, arms crossed, observing the exchange. He watched Nia ask questions, saw Leo's genuine interest in the conveyor belts, noticed Jamal's relaxed posture. His stylus moved quickly across his data pad: "Squad engaging with critical body systems. Behavior appears... educational. Subject N showing no signs of interference." He paused, stylus hovering. The sleep crew trusted these outsiders. That meant something. He filed the observation under a new category: Possible Alliance.

Leo stared at the boxes rattling past. "All that happens when I sleep?"

"Only if you actually sleep." Flo hopped onto the railing. "Skip it, and the crew never shows up. Your brain's stuck holding yesterday's junk while trying to deal with today's."

Jamal rubbed his eyes. "No wonder I bombed that vocab quiz."

A bell chimed. The lights dimmed. Velvet curtains slid down from the dome, and the whole chamber softened into twilight.

Two massive doors opened on opposite sides of the room.

The left door was carved with slow, rolling waves. The right one glittered with jagged lightning bolts.

"Two stages," Flo said. "Deep sleep and REM sleep. You cycle between them all night."

"What's the difference?" Nia asked.

"Deep sleep fixes stuff. REM sleep practices stuff." Flo pointed at the left door. "Deep is the repair crew. REM is the rehearsal studio."

Jamal perked up. "Wait. So when I dream about basketball, I'm actually practicing?"

"Your brain replays the moves, strips out the mistakes, keeps the good version." Flo nodded. "You wake up better without touching a ball."

"That's so cool," Jamal breathed.

A cold light slashed across the floor.

Leo spun around. A figure drifted in from the shadows, dragging a blade of blue-white light. It looked like a person made of screens, glowing too bright, buzzing with notifications.

The sleep crew flinched. The conveyor belts slowed. A box labeled *Algebra Steps* wobbled and nearly fell.

"The Midnight Scroller." Flo's voice went flat. "Great. Just what we needed."

The Scroller's laugh sounded like a hundred phone pings at once. "Hey, kids. One more level. One more episode. One more scroll. Who needs sleep when you've got me?"

The sleep crew covered their eyes. The belts stuttered. Boxes tipped.

"Cut it out!" Nia shouted. "You're wrecking everything!"

"Wrecking?" The Scroller's mouth stretched into a too-wide smile. "I'm keeping you entertained. Isn't that better?"

"No." Leo's fists clenched. "It's not."

The Scroller lunged forward, swinging his glowing blade. Everywhere it touched, the lights flickered and died.

The sleep crew scattered.

From the upper gallery, Agent T gripped the railing, his alert beacon glowing amber. He had called for backup twice already, finger hovering over the red emergency signal. If the Scroller destroyed the Sanctum, the entire body would suffer. But as he watched, something unexpected unfolded. The squad didn't run. They didn't hide. They strategized. Nia stepped forward with confidence, Jamal rallied beside her, and Leo stood firm. Agent T lowered the beacon. "Squad engaging hostile independently," he murmured into his comm. "Tactics appear... protective of body systems. Holding intervention." His eyes remained fixed on Nia.

Flo stepped in front of the kids. "Blue light tricks your brain into thinking it's daytime. Scares off melatonin."

"What's melatonin?" Jamal asked.

"The sleep hormone. Makes you drowsy." Flo touched her temple, and a warm amber visor shimmered over her face. Her sneakers dimmed. "No melatonin, no sleep. No sleep, no save."

A swarm of tiny, fizzing creatures poured out of a vent, buzzing like angry bees. They had neon eyes and wings that looked like soda bubbles.

"Caffeine sprites," Flo muttered. "Morning? Fine. Night? Total chaos."

The sprites swarmed the sleep crew, stuffing their fists into whistles, kicking over boxes. A crate labeled *Science Test Answers* tipped and fell.

Leo dove and caught it. "Got it!"

"Nice save!" Flo spun to face the kids. "But this is co-op. You ready?"

Leo looked at the Scroller's blade. At the swarming sprites. At the sleep crew struggling to keep the belts moving.

"Ready," he said.

"Let's do this," Nia added.

"Bring it," Jamal said.

Flo sketched three glowing circles in the air. "Three steps to beat him."

"Step one: Dim and Dock. Lower the light. Dock the devices. Tell melatonin it's safe to come back."

"Step two: Breathe and Calm. Shift from daytime to nighttime. Slow everything down."

"Step three: Routine. Same steps, same order, every night. Your brain learns the pattern."

The Scroller threw a net of glowing clips across the chamber. Tiny videos played in midair, each one ending on a cliffhanger. The sleep crew swayed, mesmerized. The belts hiccupped.

An older figure in a navy uniform stepped forward. His cap was tilted, and he carried a clipboard. He blew a low, warm note on his whistle.

The sprites scattered.

"That's Adeno," Flo said. "Boss of the sleep crew. He builds up all day, making you tired. The Scroller tries to drown him out. But tonight? We're not letting that happen."

Adeno tipped his cap. "We can keep the flow going if someone dims that glare."

Nia stepped forward. "Hey, Scroller. Wanna play a game?"

The Scroller's eyes narrowed. "What kind of game?"

"Five-step sunset. We lower every light in the room in five steps. If we win, you leave."

The Scroller smirked. "Deal."

Nia raised her hand. "Step one: Dock the devices."

A wooden charging tray appeared at the edge of the chamber. The Scroller's cloak tugged toward it. He grimaced, fighting it.

"Step two: Dim the lights."

Nia slid her hand down like turning a dial. The dome's harsh light softened to a warm glow. The Scroller's blade shrank.

"Step three: Kill the noise."

A blanket fell over the pinging notifications. They muffled to distant hums.

"Step four: Wash up."

Silver basins appeared. The kids mimed washing their faces, brushing their teeth. The caffeine sprites dove into the basins expecting fizz and wilted at the plain water.

"Step five: Story time."

Nia opened a small glowing book. She read the first line in a soft, steady voice.

The Scroller's blade flickered. His glow dimmed.

"Fine," he hissed. "You win this round. But I'll be back tomorrow night. And the night after that."

He backed into the shadows, smaller now, but still watching.

The chamber brightened.

Agent T stood slowly from his observation post, his data pad clutched in both hands. He watched the chamber restore itself, the sleep crew return to their stations, the conveyor belts hum back to life. The squad had done it. Defended critical systems. Used knowledge, not force. Worked together. His thumb hovered over the final report entry. With a decisive tap, he updated the file: "Squad status: ALLY. Recommendation: Cease surveillance. Subject N and team demonstrate clear intent to protect host systems. Request permission to offer tactical support if needed." He looked down at Nia one last time, no longer with suspicion, but with something close to respect.

A gong rolled through the hall, low and kind.

The left door opened wider. A slow river flowed in, carrying little boats with brooms and buckets. Tiny crews swept glowing dust from between twisting branches that looked like neurons.

"Glymphatic system," Flo said. "Your brain's cleaning crew. They only work during deep sleep."

Leo watched a boat glide under glowing arches. "What are they cleaning?"

"Leftover junk from the day. Waste products. Stuff that clogs up your thinking." Flo pointed at the drains where the glitter disappeared. "Skip sleep, and the junk piles up. You wake up foggy."

The gong chimed again, lighter this time.

The right door brightened. Wind chimes hummed.

"REM sleep," Flo said. "Time for rehearsal."

They stepped onto a balcony overlooking a shifting stage.

Jamal saw himself on a basketball court. Dribble, shoot, miss. Dribble, shoot, miss. Then the ball went through his legs, spun around his back, arced into the net. His form locked in.

"That's me learning," he whispered.

"Your brain's replaying the moves," Flo said. "Stripping out the bad ones, keeping the good ones. Tomorrow, your muscles will remember."

On another part of the stage, Nia saw numbers floating like fireflies. Fractions untangling. Division steps lining up. She smiled.

Leo saw himself at dinner. His mom said something sharp. His chest got tight. But dream-Leo breathed slow, counted to four, and chose a calm reply instcad.

His real shoulders loosened.

"REM helps you practice hard stuff," Flo said quietly. "Without actually breaking anything."

The stage flickered. A school hallway appeared. Someone whispered. Dream-Leo turned and walked away, laughing with his friends.

The gong called them back to the deep sleep door. The cleaning boats swept past, repair crews labeled *Recovery Mode: ON* following behind.

"If I don't sleep after practice," Jamal said slowly, "the muscles don't get fixed?"

"Exactly. You keep the damage, lose the growth." Flo nodded. "Sleep is when you actually get stronger."

Jamal crossed his arms. "I'm officially respecting bedtime."

"You'll try," Flo said, smiling.

The REM door opened again. The stage bloomed into ideas like flying. Leo learning a guitar chord, Nia filing new words next to old ones, Jamal perfecting a layup.

"Why does it switch back and forth?" Nia asked.

"Different jobs." Flo stretched. "Early in the night, you need more deep sleep for repairs. Later, you need more REM for practice. Each cycle is about ninety minutes."

The balcony brightened.

Flo clapped once. "Okay. Your turn. Walk the bridge."

A glowing path appeared:

Dock devices.

Dim lights.

Wash up.

Breathe slow.

Read something quiet.

Lights out.

They walked it together.

Nia docked an imaginary tablet. Jamal dimmed the lights with a gesture. Leo counted breaths: in for four, hold for four, out for four, hold for four. Nia read one page in a quiet voice. They tapped the switch.

The Sanctum sighed.

The deep sleep river flowed to meet them.

"What if we mess up?" Jamal asked. "Like, forget a step?"

"Do the short version," Flo said. "Dock, wash, breathe, lights out. Your body remembers the rest."

"What about nightmares?" Nia asked quietly.

"REM is practice. Sometimes practice feels scary." Flo's voice was steady. "If you wake up scared, sit up. Drink some water. Breathe squares. Tell yourself you're safe. If it keeps happening, tell an adult."

The REM door opened again.

"Pick your rehearsal," Flo said.

"Free throws," Jamal said. The stage became a gym. Breath, shoot, swish. Again. Again. The angle settled into his bones.

"Remember what I read," Nia said. Shelves appeared, glowing with new information. She sorted it, labeled it, tucked it away.

"Stay calm when kids are mean," Leo said. The hallway returned. Someone pushed him. He breathed slow and walked away. The scene dissolved.

A distant gong murmured.

The conveyor belts hummed. The sleep crew swept boxes into the archways. A star brightened above each one.

Save complete.

Adeno stamped their hands with glowing symbols: a tiny bridge, a crescent moon, a square for breathing.

"For the road," he said. "Remember the pattern."

From the shadows, a faint gleam flickered. The Scroller, smaller now but still there.

"You won this time," he whispered. "But I'll be back. And next time, you might be too tired to fight."

"Then we'll fight tired," Nia said.

The gleam faded.

Flo checked a watch only she could see. "The Sanctum will keep working till morning. But we've got other places to be."

She pointed down a tunnel glowing with warm orange light.

"Muscle Town. The repairs are already starting."

They headed toward the exit. A side room glowed as they passed, filled with tiny workers mending torn flags under a sign that read *Feelings Repair*.

Leo filed the image away for later.

"If I can't fall asleep?" Nia asked as they walked.

"Stay in bed. Breathe squares. Picture the Sanctum working. If your brain won't stop, write the thought on an imaginary card and tell yourself you'll deal with it in the morning."

"That actually helps?" Nia sounded surprised.

"Try it," Flo said.

They stepped out of the Sanctum. Behind them, the sleep crew kept working. Ahead, machines hummed.

Leo rolled his shoulders. A tiny ache that now made sense. Not damage. Promise.

"Bridge, breathe, bed," Jamal said, testing the rhythm.

"Dock, dim, dream," Nia added.

"Repair, rehearse, reset," Leo finished.

Flo's sneakers brightened. "Simple wins. Your body loves simple."

A sign ahead blinked to life: **MUSCLE TOWN - BUILDING ZONE.**

"Let's go," Leo said.

They ran toward the light.

QUESTIONS

<u>Level 4 – The Sleep Sanctum</u>

1.   What real-life habits do the Midnight Scroller and caffeine sprites represent?

2.   What makes Agent T finally call the squad "ALLY"?

3.   Why does your body need both deep sleep and REM sleep?

4.   How do screens make sleep harder?

LEVEL 5: MUSCLE TOWN
POWER PLANTS
ATP!
ATP!
ATP!
SLOW CARBS
SLOW CARBS
SLOW CARBS
SLOW CARBS
SLOW CARBS
SLOW CARBS
FAST CARBS
FAST CARBS

LEVEL 5

MUSCLE TOWN POWER PLANTS

The tunnel opened up, and sound hit them like a wave. Thump. Thump. THUMP. Not the heartbeat they'd heard before. This was different. Louder. Deeper. Like standing next to speakers at a concert. Leo stumbled forward onto a metal platform and stopped dead.

"Whoa."

Muscle Town Power Plants

Muscle Town stretched out below them. Massive towers pumped like pistons, blazing with orange and gold light. Sparks shot up conduits. The ground shook with every beat. This wasn't the quiet thinking of the brain or the gentle flow of the bloodstream. This was raw power.

"Welcome to Muscle Town!" Flo had to shout over the noise. "Your body's engine room!"

A factory door swung open below them. Dozens of tiny oval creatures marched out in formation, wearing hard hats and tool belts. Their cores shone bright yellow. They chanted like construction workers:

"ATP! ATP! Energy for you and me!"

Jamal's jaw dropped. "Are those jelly beans with jobs?"

"Mitochondria," Flo said. "Your body's power plants. They turn fuel into ATP, energy coins. No ATP, no moves."

One of the mitochondria looked up and waved. Its hard hat nearly fell off. Leo waved back, grinning.

Standing at the factory entrance, badge glowing steady green, was Agent T. No suspicion. No alert beacon. He nodded once at Nia as she passed. She blinked, surprised. He tapped his comm. "Allies confirmed in power sector. Continuing escort." His weapon stayed holstered.

They descended a ramp toward the factory floor. Conveyor belts stretched in every direction, carrying glowing crates. Some moved smooth and steady, labeled SLOW CARBS in gold letters. Others jittered and sparked, marked FAST CARBS in jittery red.

A few crates oozed grease, sliding awkwardly and leaving dark trails.

"Watch," Flo said, pointing.

A golden crate rolled into a furnace. The mitochondria opened it carefully, fed the contents in, and the whole factory blazed brighter. The chant got louder. Happier. Then a jittery red crate tumbled in.

The mitochondria dumped it. The furnace flared blindingly bright for three seconds. Then it sputtered. Dimmed. Went dark.

The mitochondria groaned. "Crash! Waste! Clean-up on lane three!"

Jamal nodded slowly. "So candy's like fireworks. Looks cool. Then you're cleaning up forever."

"Pretty much." Flo hopped onto a railing. "Your body can handle some. But too much? Everything stalls."

Nia pointed at a glowing pipe overhead labeled OXYGEN in big letters. "What's that for?"

"Hemo's crew delivers it. Red blood cells." Flo tapped the pipe. "Oxygen is the spark plug. Without it, the fuel just sits there. No burn, no energy."

Leo yawned before he could stop himself.

Flo's eyes narrowed. "How much sleep did you get last night?"

"I don't know. Maybe five hours?" Leo scratched the back of his neck. "I had to finish that raid in Star Conquerors."

"Five hours?" Nia turned on him. "Leo, that's not even close to enough."

"I'm fine," Leo snapped. "Can we just focus?"

Jamal raised his eyebrows but didn't say anything.

Flo looked like she wanted to argue, but a horn blared before she could.

Leo looked up. A greasy truck barreled down the main street, swerving wildly.

"Incoming!" Nia shouted.

"Stop it!" Flo yelled.

Leo didn't think. He just ran. Jumped onto a conveyor belt, grabbed a glowing rope of fiber, and swung it like a lasso.

The rope caught the truck's bumper. It jerked to a stop, wheels screeching, inches from the fuel line.

The mitochondria erupted in cheers. "Nice save, captain!"

Leo dropped to the ground, breathing hard. His hands shook. His legs felt rubbery. Weird. He'd sprinted for maybe ten seconds.

"That," Jamal said, "was awesome."

Flo patted Leo's shoulder. "Quick thinking. One crash like that, and the whole factory shuts down."

Agent T watched from the gantry above. His fingers flew across his data pad. Not a threat report. A commendation. He transmitted it to headquarters, then looked down at the squad. Allies protecting critical infrastructure. The immune system could learn from them.

A golden truck roared through the intersection, horn blaring. It was shaped like a banana, sparks shooting from its wheels.

"ELECTROLYTE DELIVERY!" the driver shouted. "Potassium for muscle sparks!"

The mitochondria perked up instantly. The towers surged brighter. The conveyor belts moved smoother.

Flo bounced on her toes. "Electrolytes are like jumper cables. Potassium and sodium keep the sparks firing."

"Is that why I get cramps?" Nia asked.

"Yup. Sparks misfire. Not enough potassium, too much sweat, no water." Flo made an exploding gesture. "Cramp city."

Jamal shuddered. "I got a leg cramp in the pool once. Thought a shark was eating me."

"Bananas save lives," Flo said seriously.

At the center of Muscle Town rose a massive gym. Inside, holographic muscles flexed and lifted and stretched. Every movement sent fuel surging through the towers.

"Watch this," Flo said.

Leo watched a mitochondria split in half, becoming two.

"Wait. It just made a copy of itself?"

"Movement tells your muscles to build more power plants." Flo shrugged. "Sit too long, and they retire. Use it or lose it."

Jamal poked his bicep. "I think mine already retired."

"Not permanent." Flo winked. "Move more, they come back."

Leo remembered soccer practice. Running drills. Panting. Then feeling stronger the next week. His mitochondria had been training all along.

The gym shook. A roar echoed through Muscle Town.

Something huge stomped through the factory door. It was made of wobbling jelly, spiky and dripping, with eyes that glowed sickly yellow.

"LAAAAAACTIC ACID!" it bellowed.

It slammed into a tower. Sparks flew. The conveyor belts jammed.

"Boss fight?" Leo's chest tightened.

"Mini-boss." Flo cracked her knuckles. "Lactic Acid Gremlin shows up when you push too hard without oxygen. He's not evil. Just annoying."

The gremlin threw sludge. Mitochondria collapsed, groaning. "Tired! Burn!"

"Fight back!" Flo pointed at Leo. "Breathe deep. Get oxygen flowing."

Leo inhaled. Filled his chest. The air around him shone. Oxygen bubbles streamed down the pipes into the gym.

The gremlin shrieked as the bubbles hit its sludge. It started shrinking.

Jamal grabbed a glowing water sphere and hurled it. The sludge dissolved.

Nia tossed a handful of fiber bristles. They wrapped around the gremlin like a net.

"FINE!" it squeaked, tiny now. "I'll just show up at track practice!"

It poofed into mist.

The towers flared back to life. The mitochondria cheered.

Leo bent over, hands on his knees, laughing. But his legs wobbled. His vision blurred at the edges.

"You okay?" Nia asked.

"Yeah. Just tired."

"Lactic acid leaves when oxygen flows." Flo helped him stand. "That's why warm-ups and breaks matter. You're not weak. You just need air."

They walked deeper into Muscle Town. Billboards blazed with neon slogans:

MOVE IT OR LOSE IT!
STRETCH = RECHARGE!
HYDRATE = POWER!

"I'd wear that on a shirt," Jamal muttered.

"You already are." Flo tapped his chest. "Inside."

They passed a glowing track where mitochondria sprinted laps, carrying tiny torches. Each lap sent sparks into nearby towers.

Another siren.

This time, something massive rose from the ground. It was made of couch cushions and TV static, with eyes that were dull and empty. It yawned so loud the windows rattled.

"Sedentary Sloth," Flo whispered. "Worst enemy of muscles."

The beast flopped onto a tower. The tower went dark instantly. Mitochondria collapsed, snoring.

Leo's eyelids felt heavy. The Sloth's yawn pulled at him like gravity. His knees buckled.

"Leo!" Nia grabbed his arm.

"I'm fine." But he wasn't. His whole body ached. The kind of tired that sleep couldn't fix fast.

The Sloth's voice rumbled like a lullaby. "Rest. Sleep. Give up."

Leo's eyes closed.

"Leo, wake up!" Jamal shook him.

Leo's eyes snapped open. The Sloth had spread across three towers now. Mitochondria lay scattered, snoring in piles.

Flo's face was tight with worry. "The Sloth feeds on exhaustion. You're giving it power."

"What do I do?"

"Rest." Flo pointed at a glowing chamber shaped like a bed. "Three minutes. Real rest. Let your body recharge."

"But the Sloth..."

"We'll handle it," Nia said firmly. "You can't fight tired. Trust us."

Leo wanted to argue. But his legs gave out. He stumbled into the chamber and collapsed.

The chamber hummed. Warmth spread through him. His heartbeat slowed. His breathing deepened.

Outside, Nia grabbed a jump rope that appeared at her feet. She skipped. Sparks shot out with every swing, driving the Sloth back inch by inch.

Jamal hopped onto a glowing bike and pedaled like his life depended on it. Light poured from the wheels, cutting through the static.

The Sloth shrieked. "Too much activity!"

"That's right!" Jamal shouted. "We don't need him!"

Nia glanced at the chamber. Leo's chest rose and fell, steady and deep. Three minutes. They had to hold out.

The Sloth lunged at them. Nia dodged left. Jamal swerved right. They kept moving. Kept the sparks flying.

Two minutes.

The Sloth expanded, covering four towers now. Its eyes locked on Nia. "Stop. Rest. You're so tired."

Nia's legs trembled. The jump rope slipped from her hands.

"Nia!" Jamal pedaled harder, shooting light at the Sloth's face. It recoiled, hissing.

One minute.

The chamber's glow faded. Leo's eyes opened. Clear. Focused.

He stepped out.

The Sloth turned. "You again?"

Leo smiled. "Yeah. Me again."

He ran. With every step, glowing footprints lit up the ground beneath the Sloth. Towers flickered back to life, one by one, as he passed.

"Movement wakes them up!" Flo shouted. "Keep going!"

Leo didn't feel tired anymore. He felt strong. Rested. Real rest, not just sitting still.

The Sloth screamed as light stabbed through its static body. It crumbled into dust and got sucked down a drain. The towers blazed white. The mitochondria exploded into cheers. "ATP! ATP!"

Leo stopped, breathing hard but steady. His legs didn't wobble. His vision stayed clear.

Jamal whooped. "That was insane!"

Nia wiped sweat from her forehead. "You actually rested. I didn't think you'd do it."

"I didn't think it would work." Leo flexed his fingers. "But I feel... better. Like actually better."

Flo's sneakers sparked as she walked over. "So what'd we just figure out?"

Leo thought about it. "Rest isn't weakness. It's recharging."

"And eat right," Nia added. "And move."

"Balance," Jamal said, like he'd figured out a riddle.

Agent T appeared beside Flo, silent as always. But this time he extended his hand. Leo hesitated, then shook it. Firm grip. Respectful. "The body thanks you," Agent T said. No suspicion in his voice. Just certainty. He turned to Nia last. A nod. An acknowledgment. She nodded back.

Flo pointed far ahead.

A tunnel radiated red, thumping like a warning light.

"Next stop. Your heart and arteries." Her smile faded. "And the villain waiting there? He doesn't sleep. He doesn't rest. He just squeezes."

Leo's hands went cold.

Jamal cracked his knuckles. "Bring it."

Nia pushed her glasses up. "We got this."

Leo looked at his friends. At the blazing towers behind them. At the mitochondria waving goodbye.

He rolled his shoulders. "Let's go."

Together, they stepped into the red tunnel.

The walls thumped around them.

Faster now. Harder.

And somewhere ahead, something roared.

QUESTIONS

<u>Level 5 – Muscle Town Plants</u>

1. How do mitochondria make energy for your body?

2. What is lactic acid, and why do muscles get sore?

3. What happens when you sit too much?

Level 6: Sticky Locks Crisis
O2
WHOLE FOODS
HYDRATION
MOVEMENT

LEVEL 6

THE STICKY LOCKS CRISIS

The red tunnel thumped under their sneakers, the beat heavy and fast. Leo pressed his hand against his chest. **Something pounded inside, hard and relentless, impossible to ignore.**

Ahead, the tunnel narrowed. Its glass-bright walls were lined with strange, glowing locks. Each lock flashed green when something flew past.

"What are those?" Nia squinted at the wall, adjusting her glasses.

Flo's voice dropped, serious. "Gates. They control what gets in and out."

A convoy rolled up. Some trucks gleamed, painted with bold veggies, nuts, fish. Others were boxy, greasy, splattered with fries and donut logos.

The shiny ones sailed through the locks.

The greasy ones? Not a chance. One truck spun, crashed, and exploded into gunk. Goo splattered, hardening fast across the locks.

Jamal's nose wrinkled. "Gross."

Traffic backed up. Red blood cells slammed on their brakes. Oxygen bubbles popped, bouncing off blocked lanes.

"Delivery blocked!" One cell shouted, arms thrown in the air.

Leo stared at the crusty mess. "What even is that?"

Flo stepped close, pointing. "Plaque, cholesterol build-up. Makes arteries narrow. Blood slows; heart muscles strain."

"Like clogged pipes?" Nia ventured.

"Exactly." Flo moved her hand along a wall. "Enough clogs, and...well, you get the picture."

Highway Patrol

Suddenly, a horn blared. Blue-armored HDL knights roared in on glowing bikes, swinging hooks to rip plaque away.

"Cleanup crew! Good cholesterol." Flo beamed, back to her quick self. "They haul junk to the liver for recycling."

The lead knight yanked off her helmet, face stern and tired. "Another crash. Third this hour."

Flo gestured to the squad. "Leo, Nia, Jamal, meet Commander Val. They're here to help."

Val eyed the kids, no softness at all. "Help? You're the reason we're here."

Leo blinked, taken aback. "Wait. Me?"

"This is your body," Val snapped. "Every greasy truck that crashes? Your choices. Every lock we scrub? That's overtime."

Agent T froze in the shadows, data pad clattering to the floor. Val's words echoed. Leo's body. Leo's choices. Leo causing damage. His badge flickered from green to amber.

Wrong. He'd been wrong. Leo wasn't an ally protecting systems. Leo was the host creating the chaos. Agent T's hand moved to his comm. "Surveillance team, priority alert. Target: Leo. Status: potential internal threat. Begin immediate monitoring."

Leo's face burned. "I didn't...know it worked like that."

Val didn't budge. "Didn't know or didn't care? My team's exhausted. Now you want help?"

"Not asking for help," Flo said, measured. "We're asking for a trial."

Val held her gaze, skepticism clear. "Go on."

Flo replied, "If they keep making better choices for three days, your squad barely needs to clean. If they mess up, Lock Jammer forms."

Val scanned the group, then nodded to her squad. "Three-day trial. We patrol; no cleanups. If plaque stops, we back you. If it piles up, you're on your own."

Jamal squared his stance. "What do we have to do?"

Val pulled out a tablet, tapped the screen. "Breakfast yesterday: cereal, soda. Lunch: burger, fries. Snack: chips. This is your trend." A chart spiked up in angry red.

Leo's stomach dropped.

Val continued, softer: "Today, you had oatmeal, an apple, water, and veggies. Chart's green, for now. Three more days."

Leo's hands shook, but his voice was steady. "Deal."

Val warned, "Mess up, Lock Jammer comes. He breaks the locks, and we might not stop him."

Nia leaned in to Flo. "Lock Jammer?"

Flo's sneakers dimmed. "Plaque turned monster. Enough bad choices, he'll block everything."

"I won't let that happen," Leo said, swallowing.

Val nodded. "We'll see."

The squad sped off, engines echoing.

Countdown

Flo revealed a timer. "Seventy-two hours. Let's go."

Jamal bit his lip. "What if we slip?"

Flo's reply was simple. "Every bad choice powers Lock Jammer. Old choices linger, too. The mess takes time to clear."

An ancient chip truck wobbled past, leaking sludge. It oozed onto a lock. The green glow faded.

Agent T burst from concealment, weapon drawn. Three immune sentinels materialized beside him, containment fields crackling.

"Leo, you're under arrest. Sabotaging critical systems." His voice frozen.

Leo spun, hands up. "What? No!" Nia stepped between them. Jamal grabbed Leo's shoulder.

Agent T's finger hovered over the trigger. "New sludge. More damage. You're the source."

Val skidded to a halt, eyes wide. She put her hand on Agent T's weapon, forcing it down. "Stand down, T. That sludge is two days old. From before he started fixing things."

Flo stepped forward, calm. "Past choices take time to clear. Leo's been doing everything right since the trial started. Check your own data."

Agent T's badge flickered. Amber to yellow. He pulled up his scanner, ran it over the ancient truck. Timestamp: 48 hours prior. His hand lowered. Weapon holstered. "Confirmed. Old residue." But his eyes stayed locked on Leo. "I'm watching you."

Leo whispered "That's two days old? Thank God." Heart racing. Pupils widened. Shallow breaths.

Flo nodded. "Today, you start cleaning, but yesterday's choices still count."

Nia spotted a panel, three glowing buttons: WHOLE FOODS, HYDRATION, MOVEMENT.

Flo pointed. "Press them in rhythm. Balance matters."

Leo took breakfast. Nia kept everyone hydrated. Jamal tracked movement, always reminding, "Time to get up!"

The hours ticked away. The locks glowed healthy green. Less plaque appeared. For the first time, Val's squad got ahead. No more overtime.

But at hour thirty-six, the tunnel shook. A shadow rose at the end. Massive, lumbering, chains dragging. Plaque shaped into arms and fists. Eyes burned yellow.

"Lock Jammer," Flo whispered, dread all over her face.

Leo panicked. "We did everything right!"

Flo shook her head. "Old sludge just caught up. Choices from before."

Lock Jammer roared. Locks shattered. Chaos erupted.

Val's squad shot in, swinging hooks, but Lock Jammer crashed into the wall, knocking them aside.

Flo yelled, "Three buttons! Full power! Flood the system!"

Leo, Nia, Jamal dove at the panel. "On three, one, two, three!" Slammed down.

The tunnel exploded with color: food convoys, water surges, energy flows. Locks blazed neon green.

Lock Jammer howled, scalded by the light.

Val rallied her squad, tightening hooks and hauling him back. Leo grabbed a hook, ran in. Nia threw a crate of fiber. Jamal batted a leg with a broom handle.

Plaque cracked, monster shrieked, and finally, shattered, sucked away into recycling.

Silence returned, traffic flowing smooth again.

Val strode over, a real smile on her lips. "You did it. One huge battle doesn't fix everything, but you put Lock Jammer on vacation."

Leo tried to grin, managed a wobbly smile. "So... every good choice helps."

She nodded. "And every bad one gives monsters a new job."

They fist-bumped. Nia caught her breath. Jamal muttered, "Salmon isn't so bad if it saves me from giant sludge guys."

Agent T watched from the upper corridor. Leo had fought. Defended the locks. Helped destroy the threat. His scanner showed decreasing plaque levels. Improved flow. But the data confused him. Host creating damage, then fixing it? His finger traced Leo's movement patterns. Three sentinels flanked him, waiting for orders. Agent T's badge pulsed yellow. Not green. Not red. Uncertain. He tapped a new surveillance protocol: extended monitoring, all sectors, indefinite duration. "Stay on him," he muttered. "Something doesn't add up."

Flo winked. "Ready for next level Squad?"

The billboard flickered overhead:
BALANCE FIGHTS PLAQUE: HDL HEROES, EVERY CHOICE COUNTS

Flo led them to the glowing exit. "Let's meet your body's army in Immune City. Heads up, the final boss waits for no one."

Leo tightened his backpack, felt the steady thump of a healthy heart, and stepped into white light.

QUESTIONS

<u>Level 6 – The Sticky Locks Crisis</u>

1.   What is cholesterol, and why can too much be a problem?

2.   How does HDL help protect arteries?

3.   What's the difference between healthy fats and unhealthy fats?

LEVEL 7: IMMUNE CITY – THE DEFENDERS
STEM

LEVEL 7

IMMUNE CITY: THE DEFENDERS

The white light faded. Leo blinked hard. The tunnel was gone. The ground under his feet hummed with steady purpose. The air smelled crisp and sharp, like a room after the floor's just been scrubbed with lemons.

Ahead, an arch carved with shields and swords glowed softly.

"Welcome to Immune City," Flo said, shoes glowing calm and steady. "This is your body's army."

They moved through the arch and stopped.

Agent T stood in the command tower, scanning feeds. Leo's face flashed on every monitor. Red flags pinged his system. The host. In Immune City. His headquarters. Three sentinels moved into position, weapons ready. His comm crackled. "T, do we engage?" He watched Leo look around, wide-eyed, harmless. Confused. His finger hovered over the alert. "Hold. Watch. Report every movement."

Immune City looked like a bustling fortress. On Leo's left, a honeycomb tower rose high, every window shining yellow. Conveyor belts fed pale, fresh cells stamped STEM into little chutes, names flying by faster than he could read.

"Bone Marrow Works," Flo explained. "That's where new soldiers are born."

Straight ahead, a pink fortress stood under a THYMUS PREP sign. Through its windows, caped figures sparred, bold T's blazing on their chests.

On the right, a brick wall glimmered, circled by a moat of mucus. Guards paced its top. Long fans swept dust toward hungry chutes.

Shiny rivers of silver ran everywhere, roads and currents branching to gates and checkpoints. The whole city buzzed with motion and order.

Posters shouted from the walls:
DEFENSE ISN'T LOUDEST. DEFENSE IS SMARTEST.

A siren whooped. Not wild, just controlled, like a practice drill.

Crowds funneled toward the city's center. Boxy soldiers in white jogged by, trailed by yellow-vested giants marked CLEANUP.

"What's going on?" Nia asked, a little breathless.

"Patrol," Flo said, pointing to a floating screen. It showed a huge artery wall with scratches across it. Tiny workers patched holes while greasy creatures slinked at the edges.

Leo noticed one spot pulsed red.

"Lock Jammer did that," he said quietly.

Flo nodded. "Stuff like that pops up all the time. The siren goes off, but if trouble keeps coming, no one gets to rest."

In the plaza's center stood a tower of blazing red megaphones, arms spinning, lights flashing. Every pulse sent a wave of heat across the square. More soldiers poured out.

"Inflammo," Flo muttered. "The brain of the alarm system. Alarms are good, if they turn off when they're supposed to."

A burly soldier jogged over, scuffed vest, name tag: MAC THE MACROPHAGE.

"We could use a hand," Mac rumbled. "Double alert. One's real. One's fake. My squad's wiped chasing shadows."

"Fake?" Jamal echoed, eyes wide.

Mac jerked his thumb at the main plaza. "Retired general can't tell a drill from an emergency. Third time today."

Right as he spoke, a brass band blared. A flamboyant officer spun into the square, medals clanking, baton waving. Troops rushed toward a blank spot on the wall.

"Keep up the defense! Stay sharp! Danger could be anywhere!" he shouted.

Mac groaned. "General False Alarm. My team's half-asleep because of him."

A glider swooped down as a woman stepped off, cloak branching delicately. MEMORIA - MEMORY CELL flashed on her badge. She scanned the plaza, then smiled.

"No virus," she said to Mac, handing him a glowing chip. "No bacteria. Just scuffs and grime."

"So why so much panic?" Leo asked.

Memoria tapped her head. "The general forgets which battles are worth fighting."

Mac sighed. "If we don't reset the system, real trouble could hit and we'd all miss it."

"That wall?" Nia pointed to the towering brick.

"Shield One," Mac said. "Skin, mucus, and stomach acid. The first line of defense. Keeps out the riff-raff."

"And you?"

"Shield Two. First responders," Mac flexed. "I eat bad guys and mop up messes."

Memoria nodded toward Thymus Prep. "And we train Shield Three, specialists. Custom fighters for special threats. Only send them in for the real villains."

Suddenly, a buzzer chirped from the wall. The screen showed a blue blob in a trench coat sneaking across.

Memoria laughed quietly. "Sneaky Spike. He's perfect for training."

Nia leaned close. "Training?"

Mac smiled. "Want to check out the Vaccine Vault? That's where we prep for battles before the real thing."

All three kids were instantly all in. They followed Mac and Memoria down a road lined with statues, each holding a glowing book: HOW WE WON. Boats floated silver rivers. Workers waved.

A glass dome loomed ahead: VACCINE VAULT – TRAINING ONLY.

Inside, the world hushed. Screens showed "Wanted" posters: spikes, shells, coats. Behind thick glass, robot arms presented villain pieces to soldier trainees: Y-shaped tools flying at targets.

"No full villains here," Mac explained. "Just clues. Enough to practice, then we file it for next time."

"Like practice before the big game," Jamal said.

"Exactly," Memoria replied. "I keep every record: every enemy, every trick. When it's real, we're ready."

A tall figure stepped out of a side door in blue armor, T blazing on her chest.

"T-Cell Tessa," Flo whispered.

Agent T appeared in the vault's upper gallery, invisible to trainees below. His fellow T-Cell, Tessa, showed the squad classified training protocols. Security breach. He pulled his weapon halfway. But Leo asked questions. Smart ones. About defense. About preparation. Nia took notes. Jamal listened, focused. They weren't sabotaging. They were learning. His weapon slid back. Badge flickered yellow again. Still watching.

Tessa raised her visor. "Trainees are sharp; memories loaded. We're on watch for the real thing."

A cheerful guy rolled in with a cart of gleaming Y's. BENNY - ANTIBODY WORKS.

"Ten thousand finished!" he sang. "Each fits one enemy, no mix-ups allowed."

"Like glue guns for germs," Jamal laughed.

Benny beamed. "Exactly!"

Tessa pointed to a display. "Every cell wears a Self Badge. If you've got the badge, you're safe. If not, we check."

Nia asked, "What if you make a mistake?"

Memoria's voice softened. "Then we cause trouble by accident, so we double-check everything."

Flo nodded. "Let's head back. We've got a siren to fix."

Flo hustled Leo, Nia, and Jamal out of the Vaccine Vault and back into Immune City's main plaza. The fake alarms still echoed, but Mac barked orders, trying to keep the squads focused.

A stream of workers hurried past, checking badges and gear. Suddenly, one smaller cell tripped, dropping a stack of Self Badges all over the floor. Jamal bent down to help, stacking them into a neat pile.

Memoria watched, nodding. "A good helper sticks to the record books. That way, the right cells get through, and mistakes stay small."

Across the square, General False Alarm whipped the crowd into another panic drill, baton hitting the air with each sharp word. But real trouble was brewing. At the edge of the city, three greasy blobs snuck in, aiming for the main artery.

Flo pointed. "Trouble. Not a drill."

Mac dove forward, leading first responders. Nia tugged Leo's sleeve. "Should we help?"

Leo's heart raced. "We're here, aren't we?"

Jamal gulped, but squared his shoulders. "Like real soldiers."

The kids grabbed mop-tools again and joined the clean-up crew. Leo tackled one greasy blob, his arms shaking, but determination rising. Jamal flanked another, knocking it into the Clean-Up Giant's bucket. Nia ran data to Memoria, who tracked every movement, shouting out advice.

The city pulsed with teamwork. Some cells patched up holes, others watched the front lines.

Then, all at once, the loud alarm stopped. The red megaphones dimmed. False Alarm watched as Mac, Memoria, the trainees, and the kids finished the real mess, faster, smarter, confident.

Flo high-fived the squad. "You figured out what matters. Less panic, more precision."

Mac rumbled, "Even generals can learn. You three are official squad helpers."

In the command towers, a shadow of Agent T showed his weapon was holstered. Leo tackled a greasy blob. Jamal knocked another into containment. Nia ran data straight to Memoria without hesitation. The numbers didn't lie. Squad helped. Real threat eliminated. He tapped his badge twice, logging the report: "Cleared for city access."

Memoria handed each of them a glowing chip. "It's a memory boost. For days you forget what you did, and who you helped."

Leo pocketed his chip, feeling a small but powerful sense of pride.

As the sky overhead shifted from bright yellow to peaceful blue, Flo led the squad toward the city gates.

"Next level's waiting," she whispered.

QUESTIONS

<u>Level 7 – Immune City: The Defenders</u>

1.   What is Mac's job in defending the body?

2.   How does the immune system "remember" germs?

3.   How do vaccines train the immune system?

LEVEL 8: THE PRESSURE BEAST
DANGER
DANGER
DANGER
DANGER
DANGER
JAMAL
23

LEVEL 8

THE PRESSURE BEAST

The ramp shook beneath their sneakers. Red lights pulsed along canyon walls, matching a giant heartbeat. Leo, Nia, and Jamal stepped into a world of living arteries, walls flexing and glowing with each beat. It should've been incredible. However, something was wrong.

Where traffic once flowed fast and clear, everything jammed up. Red blood cells honked, oxygen bubbles wobbled. Vitamins boxed in. Plasma crawled thick as syrup.

Groans echoed at every pulse. Pipes strained, Heart work under siege.

Flo darted ahead, sparks flying from her sneakers, her usual cheer traded for focus. "Welcome to Level Eight:

Avalanche Zone. Arteries are supposed to be superhighways. Now? Avalanche warning."

The squad peered over the rail. Chunks of nasty plaque jutted out, yellow-brown like old gum. Big LDL trucks dumped greasy loads, piling chaos on the walls. HDL knights zoomed in to help, but couldn't keep up.

Nia gulped, eyes wide. "This looks disastrous."

Flo nodded. "Narrow lanes mean higher pressure. That's danger territory."

Agent T crouched at a maintenance hatch, badge glowing red. Plaque everywhere. LDL trucks dumping more. He scanned the squad. Leo touched the artery wall, reading the pulse. Nia calculated pressure ratios on her tablet. Jamal mapped escape routes. Still helpful. Badge flickered orange. He logged coordinates, then vanished into the shadows.

The ground rumbled. A roar rolled through the artery.

"If pressure rises too high," Flo called, "the Pressure Beast wakes up."

From the tunnel's deepest shadows, a hulking creature stomped forward. Pipes burst from its shoulders, rusty clamps armor its chest, chains drag behind. Steam hissed from its nose, and red eyes flashed.

Pressure Beast.

Leo pressed his hand to the wall and felt it throb. Hot and angry. His own pulse sped up, syncing with the chaos.

"Definitely worse than Lock Jammer," he muttered.

Pressure Beast slammed fists into walls. Cracks split, oxygen bubbles popped, vitamins tumbled everywhere.

"He feeds on stress, salt, grease, and sitting still!" Flo shouted. "Bad habits make him strong. If the avalanche gets too big: heart attack. Stroke."

Jamal's face went pale. "My health class nightmare, live and oversized."

The beast bellowed, "MORE PRESSURE! MORE POWER!"

Leo's voice squeaked. "We can beat this. Right?"

Nia's hands shook, but she nodded. Jamal's answer was barely a squeak, "Uh...sure."

A control panel glinted on the wall, HYDRATION.

Leo slapped the button. Water rushed in. Blood cells surged. Traffic eased a little.

Nia scrambled up to another console, pushing MIND-FUL BREATHING. The artery inhaled deeply, exhaled. For a second, calm swept through.

"That's it!" Flo cheered. "Deep breathing can lower stress!"

But the beast wasn't done.

Chains smashed walls, plaque chunks blocked the path. Ahead, a monster clot rolled forward, getting bigger, sucking up debris.

"Clot avalanche!" Flo's voice cracked. "If that blocks the flow, it's game over!"

Leo glanced at the panel, the beast, the clot. Buttons weren't stopping it.

"We need a new plan," he said.

"What kind of plan?" Jamal asked, voice shaky.

Leo looked at the HDL knights clearing plaque, the clot growing near a bottleneck. "We have to stop the clot before it jams up the artery. Nia, keep the breathing steady. Jamal, you're with me."

"I have no idea what we're doing," Jamal admitted. "Let's find out."

They dashed toward the clot. Up close, it was a tangled, sticky mess, a rolling disaster of plaque and fibers.

"How do we fight this?!" Jamal yelled.

HDL knights tried lassoing the clot but it was too heavy.

Leo pointed. "Break it into smaller pieces! Can you help?"

A knight handed Leo a glowing Omega-3 blade. "Cut through the sticky strands. The pieces will break free."

Leo took a breath and climbed onto the clot with Jamal. It squished and sucked, but Leo sliced at the glowing bonds. Chunks peeled off, breaking away.

"It's working!" Jamal shouted.

Suddenly, Pressure Beast whipped a chain at the wall above them. Debris rained down.

"Leo!" Nia screamed from above.

"Jump!" Jamal cried.

They leapt off the clot, just in time. Debris smashed into the mass, cracking it apart. HDL knights rushed in, dragging pieces to be recycled.

From his observation point on the platform, Agent T watched, weapons drawn. Leo and Jamal climbed the clot. Sliced through fibers. Broke it apart. Nia kept systems calm above. Squad worked together. No chaos. No sabotage. Badge pulsed yellow, then pale green. He holstered one weapon. Kept watching.

Leo collapsed, covered in plaque. "Did that really just work?"

Jamal wheezed, "We didn't die. That counts."

Flo skated over, inspecting the scene. "Not bad. Pressure Beast isn't gone, but the blockage is."

Pressure Beast stomped closer, walls shaking. Chains rattled. The artery shuddered.

Leo checked the control panels: Hydration. Breathing. Movement. All activated. Not enough.

"What else can calm pressure?" Flo prompted.

Leo thought of traffic jams, stressy mornings, endless late-night pushes. "Rest," he said, barely audible.

Nia blinked. "Rest? Now?"

Flo nodded. "Pressure feeds off going nonstop. Rest cuts it down."

Leo closed his eyes, loosened his shoulders, let out a long breath. Artery walls softened, heartbeat slowed.

Blue mist drifted down, melatonin, cooling the chaos.

Pressure Beast dropped to his knees. Chains slipped away. He shrank. Smaller, then melted into the ground.

The artery glowed pink; blood cells sped by. Oxygen bubbles sparkled like victory confetti.

Leo lay back, exhausted but steady.

Jamal groaned, "My new hobby? Sleep. Like, forever."

Nia sat nearby, glasses askew. "We fought a giant made of stress and salt. Real hero stuff."

Flo smiled wide, helping Leo up. "Every healthy choice: less salt, more water, breathing, moving, real rest, shrinks the Beast."

Nia adjusted her glasses. "Little habits, big shields."

Flo pointed at the bike-riding HDL knight. "Thank your captain, he led the charge!"

The knight saluted. "Teamwork wins."

Stepping from the shadows, shocked, both weapons lowered, Agent T spoke. "Pressure Beast melted. Artery clear. Squad rested, exhausted but victorious." Leo chose rest over pressure. Smart. Badge glowed steady green. He tapped twice, updating the file: "Squad understands balance. Not saboteurs. Allies, at least for now." He turned and followed them still. Nia's mirror eyes – glasses turned to be nothing. Leo's sludge was history. Does Jamal have anything to be worried about? Maybe not, follow anyway, but hopeful.

Flo gestured ahead. Rainbow swirls shimmered beyond the tunnel. "Next stop: Emergency Response Zone. Get ready for a wild ride."

Leo straightened, steadier this time.

"Squad, you in?" he asked.

Nia punched Jamal's arm. "Always."

Jamal nodded. "Bring it."

They stepped forward into the storm of color, ready for what was next.

QUESTIONS

<u>Level 8 – The Pressure Beast</u>

1.   What makes blood pressure go up? Why is very high pressure dangerous?

2.   How can stress change blood pressure?

3.   What are some healthy ways to keep pressure in a safe range?

AMYGDALA
STRESS HORMONES
STRESS HORMONES
PANIC GREMLIN
IMAGINE THOUGHTS
4
7
8

LEVEL 9

EMERGENCY RESPONSE ZONE

The rainbow portal spun them out like a carnival ride. Leo landed first, knees buckling, breath knocked loose. Nia tumbled after him, glasses askew. Jamal hit the platform last, groaning.

"Where are we now?" Leo wheezed.

Flo's sneakers sparked as she landed beside them. But this time, something was wrong. Her glow flickered. Dimmed. Like a dying flashlight.

Nia pushed herself up. "Flo, are your sneakers..."

"I'm fine." Flo's voice came out sharp. Too sharp. "Just tired. We need to move."

But she swayed. Caught herself on the railing.

"You're not fine," Leo said.

"I said I'm FINE." Flo turned away. "Welcome to the Emergency Response Zone. We need to focus."

The platform beneath them thrummed. Not steady like a heartbeat, but fast. Frantic. Like drums beating too quick, over and over, never slowing down.

Leo stood and looked around.

The Emergency Response Zone

The walls pulsed red. Sirens wailed in the distance. Alarm lights flashed everywhere. The air tasted sharp and metallic, like the moment before lightning strikes.

"Something's wrong," Nia whispered. "Really wrong."

They walked to the edge of the platform and peered down into a massive control room. Workers dashed back and forth, adrenal glands shaped like little kidneys with legs, their faces tight with panic. They hauled buckets labeled ADRENALINE and CORTISOL, dumping them into glowing chutes that sent the hormones racing through the body.

"Why are they dumping so much?" Jamal asked.

"Because the body thinks it's in danger," Flo said. Her voice was quieter now. "Real, life-or-death danger."

Leo frowned. "But I'm not being chased by a bear."

"Your body doesn't know that." Flo looked away. "Stress from school, fighting with friends, worrying about tests... your body can't tell the difference. So it sounds the alarms anyway."

She paused.

"And if the alarms never stop..."

Agent T watched from a maintenance walkway above. Badge flickered yellow. Emergency Response Zone meant real danger. Cortisol flooding. Adrenaline pumping. But no bear. No attacker. Just fear. He scanned the squad. Leo frowned, piecing it together. Nia whispered concerns. Jamal looked rattled. They saw the problem. Badge pulsed amber. This wasn't sabotage. This was learning.

A shadow moved through the control room. Tall. Jagged. Made of twisted metal chains, crackling lightning, and storm clouds that hissed with every step.

Its voice came from everywhere at once. A thousand whispers overlapping.

"What if you fail what if they laugh what if you're not good enough what if something bad happens what if what if what if..."

Leo's hands went cold and sweaty at the same time. His stomach twisted. His thoughts raced so fast he couldn't catch one before the next came.

This was how he felt before every test. Every presentation. Every time he had to meet someone new.

"The Anxiety Titan," Flo whispered.

The Titan had too many arms, each one gripping a different part of the control room: squeezing the heart, tightening around the lungs, wrapping around the stomach.

A monitor on the wall blazed red:

HEART RATE: 120 BPM
BREATHING: SHALLOW AND QUICK
BLOOD PRESSURE: RISING
MUSCLES: LOCKED TIGHT
STOMACH: KNOTTED
IMMUNE SYSTEM: SHUTTING DOWN

"That's how I feel before a big test," Leo said.

"Exactly," Flo said. "The Anxiety Titan turns on your fight-or-flight system. That's helpful if there's a real threat. But if it stays on all the time? Your body gets exhausted. Your immune system stops working. You get sick. Your stomach hurts. You can't sleep."

Nia clutched her stomach. "My cousin gets stomachaches every Monday before school."

"That's the Titan," Flo said.

The Anxiety Titan slammed one massive fist into the floor. The entire platform shook. Workers stumbled, dropping their buckets. Cortisol and adrenaline spilled everywhere, flooding the control room in a toxic wave.

"We have to stop him," Leo said.

Flo pointed to three glowing stations around the room, but her hand trembled.

"Breath Regulator. Movement Engine. Rest Chamber." Her voice was barely audible. "Activate them. Calm the Titan."

"What about you?" Jamal asked. "You look..."

"I'm FINE," Flo snapped. Then, softer, "Just go. Please."

Leo hesitated. But the Titan roared, and the workers screamed.

"Okay," he said. "Nia, take the Breath Regulator. Jamal, Movement Engine. I'll handle Rest."

They nodded and split up.

The Breath Regulator

Nia sprinted to the Breath Regulator. Two giant lungs glowed soft blue, rising and falling in a slow, steady rhythm.

A control panel blinked in front of her. Three buttons. Three different breathing patterns.

Which one was right?

Her heart hammered. If she chose wrong, the Titan would grow stronger. If the Titan grew stronger, they'd all die. If they died, it would be her fault.

Her hands shook.

"Just pick one," she whispered. "Just pick the right one. Don't mess up. Don't mess up don't mess up don't..."

Her breath came faster. Shorter.

The room tilted.

What if I pick wrong? What if I kill everyone? What if I'm not smart enough? What if what if what if...

The Anxiety Titan's whispers wrapped around her like chains.

Nia couldn't breathe.

She pressed her hands to her chest. Gasped. But no air came.

"Nia!" Leo shouted from across the room. "Hit the button!"

But she couldn't move. Couldn't think. Couldn't breathe.

The monitor on the wall flashed:

**PANIC ATTACK IN PROGRESS
HYPERVENTILATION DETECTED
OXYGEN LEVELS DROPPING**

Jamal looked up from the Movement Engine. "What's happening to her?!"

"She's spiraling," Flo said. Her sneakers barely glowed now. "The Titan's got her."

"We have to help her!" Jamal started toward Nia.

"No!" Flo grabbed his arm. "If you leave the Movement Engine, the Titan grows. If he grows, Leo's heart could stop."

Having emerged from the shadows, Agent T had his weapon drawn. Nia gasping. Leo's heart spiking. Titan crushing everything. He aimed at the Titan, but hesitated. Not a physical threat. Mental. Emotional. Can't shoot fear. Badge flickered red, then yellow. Leo chose to help Nia instead of protecting himself. Squad risked everything for each other. Badge steadied to pale green. He lowered his weapon.

Leo froze at the Rest Chamber. "What?"

"The Titan's squeezing your heart right now," Flo said. "The only thing keeping it beating is the work you're all doing. If even one of you stops..."

The monitor flashed again:

LEO - HEART RATE: 140 BPM
CRITICAL THRESHOLD APPROACHING

Leo's chest tightened. He could feel it now. The pressure. Like an invisible hand squeezing.

Jamal looked at Nia. At Leo. At the Titan.

"What do we do?!" His voice cracked.

Flo swayed. Her sneakers flickered once. Twice.

And went out.

She collapsed.

The Choice

Leo ran to Flo. Caught her before she hit the ground.

"Flo! FLO!"

Her eyes fluttered open. Barely. "I'm sorry," she whispered. "I thought... I thought if I just ate less... stayed smaller... the bosses wouldn't be so scary. If I controlled everything... I wouldn't feel so out of control."

Her voice broke.

"But I can't help you now. I'm too weak."

Leo's throat tightened. "You have an eating disorder?"

"I'm the expert," Flo whispered. "I'm supposed to know better. But knowing doesn't... doesn't always fix it."

Her eyes closed.

Leo looked around.

Nia was on the ground, hyperventilating, tears streaming down her face.

Jamal was frozen at the Movement Engine, looking back and forth between his friends.

The Anxiety Titan was growing. His chains tightened around the heart monitor. Around the lungs. Around everything.

LEO - HEART RATE: 150 BPM
DANGER: CARDIAC EVENT IMMINENT

If Leo went to help Nia, he'd leave the Rest Chamber. The Titan would crush his heart.

If Jamal went to help Nia, he'd leave the Movement Engine. The cortisol would flood unchecked.

But if they did nothing, Nia would pass out. Maybe worse.

"What do we do?!" Jamal shouted.

Leo's mind raced. His hands shook. His chest squeezed tighter.

Then he remembered.

The Sleep Sanctum. The pledge.

I will breathe the sirens down when they're too loud.

"Jamal!" Leo shouted. "Stay at the Engine! Keep moving!"

"But Nia..."

"I'm going to her!"

"Your heart..."

"I know!" Leo's voice cracked. "But she needs help NOW. If I stay here doing nothing while she's drowning, what's the point of any of this?!"

He left the Rest Chamber and ran.

The monitor screamed:

LEO - HEART RATE: 160 BPM
CRITICAL DANGER

The Anxiety Titan roared. His chains tightened. Leo's chest felt like it was being crushed in a vice.

But he kept running.

He dropped to his knees beside Nia.

"Nia! Look at me!"

She couldn't. Her eyes were wide and unfocused. Gasping. Sobbing.

"Nia, I need you to breathe with me. Can you do that?"

She shook her head frantically.

"Yes you can," Leo said. His own voice was shaking. His own chest was tightening. But he kept going. "Four counts. In. Hold. Out. Hold. Like we learned in the Sleep Sanctum. Remember?"

He breathed. Slow and steady.

"In... two... three... four..."

Nia gasped. Choked.

"Hold... two... three... four..."

She tried. Failed. Gasped again.

Leo kept breathing.

"Out... two... three... four..."

Nia's breath came out ragged. But longer than before.

"Hold... two... three... four..."

She matched him. Just barely.

"Again," Leo said. "In... two... three... four..."

The Anxiety Titan's whispers grew louder.

"She's weak she's failing it's your fault you're not good enough..."

"Shut up," Leo said.

He looked Nia in the eyes.

"You're not weak. You're not failing. You made one mistake. One. And that's okay. We're going to fix it together."

Nia's breath steadied. Just a little.

"One more time," Leo said. "In... two... three... four..."

They breathed together.

Slowly, Nia's color came back. Her hands stopped shaking.

"I'm sorry," she whispered.

"Don't be sorry. Just breathe."

She nodded.

They stood. Together. Leo's legs wobbled. His chest still felt like it was being crushed.

But they walked to the Breath Regulator.

"Which button?" Nia asked, voice still shaking.

Leo looked at the panel. Three buttons. Three patterns.

"I don't know," he admitted. "But we'll figure it out. Try the middle one."

Nia pressed it.

The giant lungs inflated. Slow. Steady. Deep.

A wave of soft blue light rippled through the control room.

The Anxiety Titan flinched. His lightning arms flickered.

"It's working!" Jamal shouted from the Movement Engine.

But Leo collapsed.

The Final Push

"LEO!" Nia screamed.

He was on the ground, clutching his chest, gasping.

The monitor flashed:

LEO - HEART RATE: 170 BPM
CARDIAC ARREST IMMINENT

Nia looked at the Rest Chamber. Then at Leo. Then at the Titan.

"Jamal! Keep moving!"

"What are you doing?!" Jamal shouted.

"What Leo did for me!"

She dragged Leo toward the Rest Chamber. He was heavy. Too heavy. But she didn't stop.

The Titan's chains reached for them. Lightning crackled.

Nia shoved Leo into the Rest Chamber.

Above him, stars twinkled. A soft hum filled the air.

But Leo's eyes were closed. His breathing shallow.

"Leo, please," Nia whispered. "Rest. Just rest."

She climbed in beside him. Held his hand.

"You're safe," she said. "Right here. Right now. You're safe."

The stars brightened. Warmth spread through the chamber.

Leo's breathing slowed. Deepened.

His eyes opened.

"Nia?"

"You're okay," she said. Relief flooded her voice. "You're okay."

The blue light from the Breath Regulator mixed with the yellow sparks from the Movement Engine. Together, they swirled around the Anxiety Titan like warm fog.

He stumbled. His lightning dimmed. His storm clouds thinned.

"Rest... makes me... weak..."

"No," Leo said, voice hoarse. "Rest is when the body heals. When the alarms finally turn off. When you remember you're safe."

The Anxiety Titan shrank. Smaller. Smaller. His chains loosened and fell away.

And then, with one final sigh, he dissolved into mist.

The sirens stopped.

The red lights faded to calm amber.

The workers put down their buckets and sat, exhausted but smiling.

He holstered his weapon completely. Agent T had seen enough: Titan dissolved. Alarms stopped. Squad helped each other through panic, sacrifice, mental crisis. Leo risked his heart to save Nia. Nia dragged Leo to safety. Flo revealed her struggle. This wasn't physical combat. This was emotional warfare. Badge glowed bright green. He updated the file: "Squad proven. Allies confirmed. Mental health matters." He would follow them to the end.

The monitor updated:

HEART RATE: 70 BPM
BREATHING: DEEP AND STEADY
BLOOD PRESSURE: NORMAL
MUSCLES: RELAXED
IMMUNE SYSTEM: ACTIVE

Leo climbed out of the Rest Chamber. His legs were steady.

Nia wiped tears from her face. "I almost got you killed."

"No," Leo said. "You saved me. Just like I helped you."

Jamal ran over. "That was the scariest thing I've ever seen."

They hugged. All three of them. Shaking. Crying a little. But okay.

A soft glow appeared behind them.

Flo.

Her sneakers sparked. Faint, but there.

"You did it," she whispered.

"Are you okay?" Nia asked.

Flo shook her head. "No. But I will be. I need help. Real help. Not just knowing what to do, but actually doing it."

She looked at Leo. "Thank you. For showing me that asking for help isn't weakness."

Leo nodded. "We all need help sometimes."

Flo's sneakers brightened. Just a little.

A new portal shimmered open ahead, glowing soft green.

"What's next?" Jamal asked.

Flo took a shaky breath. "Level Ten. And trust me... you're gonna meet some real warriors."

Leo breathed. Slow and steady.

"Squad," he said. "Let's go."

Together, they stepped into the green light.

QUESTIONS

<u>Level 9 – Emergency Response Zone</u>

1.   How can anxiety feel in your body?

2.   How is a panic attack different from feeling nervous?

3.   Why was it brave for Flo to share her eating disorder story?

4.   What's the difference between feeling anxious and having an anxiety disorder?

GUT
GALAXY
JAMAL

LEVEL 10
THE GUT GALAXY

The portal spun them out into a world that smelled like warm bread, pickles, and something faintly sour. Leo landed on soft ground that bounced beneath his feet. Nia tumbled after him, glasses askew. Jamal hit last, groaning.

"Where are we now?" Leo asked.

He looked up.

And his jaw dropped.

Gut Galaxy

Above them, planets whirled in orbit, connected by glowing highways. Some worlds sparkled gold and clean. Others dripped with green slime. Tiny creatures drifted through the air like fireflies. Some friendly and round, others sharp and slithering.

The whole place felt alive. Buzzing. Humming. Like standing inside a beehive made of food.

Flo landed beside them, but her sneakers barely sparked. She swayed, caught herself on Leo's shoulder.

"Flo?" Nia's voice was small.

"I'm okay." Flo's voice was quiet. "Still recovering. But I'm here."

She straightened, took a breath, and gestured around them.

"Welcome to Gut Galaxy. Where trillions of microbes keep your body running."

Jamal stared. "Wait, so my belly is basically Star Wars, but with snacks?"

"Exactly," Flo said. A small smile crossed her face. "And right now? The galaxy's at war."

Leo looked closer. The golden planets were surrounded by tiny creatures wearing what looked like yogurt capes, waving bean flags. They bounced and sang, voices high and cheerful.

But on the darker planets, greasy creatures in slick armor slithered through the slime, leaving trails of gunk on the highways.

"The good guys are probiotics," Flo said. "They help digest food, protect your immune system, even control your mood. Feed them fiber, and they thrive."

She pointed at the slime-covered planets.

"The bad guys are harmful bacteria. Feed them too much junk food, and they take over. When the balance tips too far..."

The ground beneath them shook.

A massive shadow rose from the center of the galaxy. Tall. Wrapped in armor made of grease and sugar crystals. Eyes blazing yellow.

A voice boomed across Gut Galaxy.

"KIDS CRAVE ME! SODA! CANDY! FRIES! I RULE HERE!"

"Toxina," Flo whispered. "Queen of Chaos."

Toxina slammed her fists into the ground. Slime exploded outward in waves.

"What happens if she wins?" Nia asked.

Flo's face was grim. "If the harmful bacteria take over completely? Your gut shuts down. Either explosive diarrhea flushes everything out, good and bad. Or the system locks up in constipation so bad nothing moves. Either way..."

"We die," Leo finished.

"Yeah," Flo said.

A roar echoed across the galaxy. Toxina's army swarmed out from the dark planets. Grease Goblins riding burger hovercrafts. Sugar Slimes giggling and sticky. Bad Bacteria waving soda straw spears.

They surrounded the golden planets. The probiotics tried to fight back, but they were outnumbered.

"We have to help them!" Jamal shouted.

"Wait." Flo grabbed his arm. Her hand shook. "This isn't like the other battles. You can't just throw items and press buttons. Toxina feeds on cravings. The more you want junk food, the stronger she gets."

Leo's stomach twisted. "So how do we beat her?"

"You have to resist," Flo said. "Actually resist. She's going to offer you everything you've ever craved. And you have to say no."

Nia swallowed. "All of us?"

"All of you," Flo said. "Together. If even one of you gives in, she wins."

The ground shook again. Toxina turned toward them. Her eyes locked on.

"NEW PLAYERS," she boomed. "WELCOME. ARE YOU HUNGRY?"

The Temptation

Toxina raised her arms. The air shimmered.

Suddenly, a table appeared in front of Leo. Covered with everything he'd ever wanted. Hot pizza with extra cheese. A mountain of chips. Ice-cold soda in huge cups. Candy bars stacked like treasure.

His mouth watered. His stomach growled.

"You've been working so hard," Toxina's voice purred. "You deserve a reward. Just one bite. What's the harm?"

Leo reached out. His hand shook.

"Leo, don't!" Nia shouted.

But then another table appeared in front of her. Cookies. Brownies. Chocolate cake with thick frosting. All her favorites.

"You're so stressed," Toxina whispered. "Always trying to be perfect. Always worrying. This will make you feel better. Just for a moment."

Nia's hand moved toward a cookie.

"Nia!" Jamal yelled.

But a third table appeared in front of him. Burgers. Fries. Milkshakes. Everything he'd eaten at his birthday party last year.

"You're strong," Toxina said. "One burger won't hurt. You'll just exercise it off tomorrow. You always do."

Jamal grabbed a burger.

Lifted it to his mouth.

Stopped.

He looked at Leo. At Nia. At Flo, swaying on her feet, barely able to stand.

"This is what she did to you, isn't it?" Jamal asked Flo quietly. "Made you think that less was better. That control meant safety."

Flo's eyes filled with tears. She nodded.

Jamal put the burger down. "I'm not giving her that power."

Leo's hand was still reaching for the pizza. But he stopped. Pulled back.

"Every time I ate this stuff, I felt good for like five minutes," he said. "Then I felt worse. Tired. Foggy. Cranky."

He stepped away from the table. "I don't want to feel like that anymore."

Nia stared at the cookies. Her favorite cookies. The ones her mom made when she was sad.

But these weren't from her mom. These were from Toxina.

"Food isn't the enemy," Nia said quietly. "But using it to hide from feelings? That doesn't help."

She turned away from the table.

Agent T stepped into view. All three resisted. Leo walked away from pizza. Jamal put down the burger. Nia turned from cookies. No hesitation. No failure. Badge blazed green. He tapped his report: "Squad passed final test. Mental strength proven. Mission complete."

Toxina shrieked. "NO! YOU'RE SUPPOSED TO CHOOSE ME!"

The tables vanished.

But Toxina wasn't done.

The Real Battle

"Fine," Toxina snarled. "If you won't choose me willingly, I'll MAKE you."

She raised her arms. The harmful bacteria swarmed the probiotics. The golden planets started to go dark.

"The probiotics are losing!" Flo gasped. "Without balance, they can't fight back!"

"What do we do?!" Leo shouted.

"Feed them!" Flo pointed at crates scattered around the galaxy. "Fiber! Healthy fats! Variety! But you have to get to them!"

Leo looked at the battlefield. Grease Goblins blocked the paths. Sugar Slimes covered the crates. Bad Bacteria guarded every route.

"We'll have to go through them," he said.

"Together," Nia added.

"Squad up," Jamal said.

They ran.

Leo dodged a Grease Goblin and grabbed a crate labeled BEANS. He hurled it toward the nearest golden planet. Probiotics caught it, tore it open, and devoured the contents. They glowed brighter. Stronger.

Nia found a crate marked APPLES. She dragged it, but a Sugar Slime wrapped around her leg.

"Jamal!"

Jamal kicked the Slime away. Together, they pushed the crate to another planet. More probiotics powered up.

But Toxina wasn't just standing there.

She grabbed one of the golden planets and squeezed. The probiotics inside screamed.

"STOP!" Leo yelled.

"Feed me or I crush them all!" Toxina roared. "Give in to the cravings!"

Leo's hands balled into fists. "Never."

He spotted a massive crate in the center of the battlefield. Bigger than all the others. Labeled FERMENTED FOODS.

"That one!" Flo pointed, breathless. "That's the power-up. Sauerkraut. Kimchi. Yogurt. If the probiotics get that, they can fight back!"

"How do we get it to them?" Nia asked.

The crate was surrounded. Dozens of enemies. No clear path.

Leo looked at his friends. At Flo, barely standing but refusing to give up.

"We don't carry it," Leo said. "We become the path."

"What?" Jamal blinked.

"Line up. Shoulder to shoulder. We push through together. They can't stop all of us at once."

Nia adjusted her glasses. "That's either brilliant or really stupid."

"Probably both," Leo admitted. "But it's all we've got."

They linked arms. Flo too, weak but determined.

"On three," Leo said. "One. Two. THREE!"

They charged.

Grease Goblins bounced off them. Sugar Slimes tried to wrap around their legs, but they kept moving. Bad Bacteria swung their spears, but the kids ducked and pushed forward.

They reached the crate.

Together, they shoved it toward the largest golden planet.

Probiotics poured out. Grabbed the crate. Ripped it open.

And ate.

The Turning Point

The change was instant.

The probiotics glowed so bright it hurt to look at them. They grew. Multiplied. Surged out across the galaxy in waves of golden light.

The Grease Goblins melted. The Sugar Slimes popped. The Bad Bacteria scattered, fleeing back to their dark planets.

Toxina stumbled. "No. NO! I am your CRAVINGS! You can't resist me!"

"We just did," Leo said.

The probiotics surrounded Toxina. Not attacking. Just standing there. Glowing. Balanced.

"You're not gone forever," Nia said. "Cravings happen. But they don't have to control us."

Toxina shrank. Smaller. Smaller. Until she was no bigger than a marble.

A probiotic in a yogurt cape picked her up gently and placed her in a small containment pod.

"She'll be back," the probiotic said. His voice was kind. "But as long as you maintain balance, she'll stay small."

The probiotic wore a crown made of sauerkraut. King Probiotic.

"Thank you," he said, bowing. "You saved Gut Galaxy."

Leo felt his knees buckle. He sat down hard. "That was terrifying."

"That was the hardest one yet," Jamal agreed.

Nia was shaking. "I almost ate that cookie."

"But you didn't," Flo said quietly. She sat beside them, exhausted but smiling. "None of you did. You chose balance."

"So did you," Leo said. "You could've stayed behind. Rested. But you came anyway."

Flo's eyes got wet. "I'm still learning. Just like you."

They sat together for a moment. Breathing. Recovering.

Around them, Gut Galaxy sparkled. Healthy. Balanced. Alive.

Going Home

A portal shimmered into view. Not glowing like the others. Just... normal. Real.

Words appeared above it: HOME BASE - IRL.

Leo looked at it. Then at his friends. Then at Flo.

"So this is it?" he asked.

Flo nodded. "This is it. But it's also just the beginning."

"What happens when we go back?" Nia asked.

"You live what you learned," Flo said. "Small choices. Every day. That's how you keep the balance."

Leo took a breath. He felt different. Not just stronger. Clearer. Like he finally understood how his body worked. How to listen to it. How to help it.

"Will we see you again?" Jamal asked.

Flo smiled. "Maybe. When you need a reminder. Or when I need one."

She stood, steadier now than when they'd arrived.

"Thank you," she said. "For reminding me that even guides need help sometimes."

Leo stood too. "Thanks for showing us how our bodies work. For being honest. Even when it was hard."

Nia and Jamal stood beside him.

"Squad ready?" Leo asked.

They nodded.

Together, the three kids stepped toward the portal.

Leo paused at the threshold. Turned back.

"Hey, Flo?"

She looked up.

"Keep fighting," Leo said. "You've got this."

Flo's sneakers sparked bright. Just for a moment.

"So do you," she said.

Leo smiled.

Then he stepped through the portal with his friends.

Into the light.

Into the real world.

Ready.

Agent T watched from the portal's edge. Squad stepped through. Returning home. Ten levels completed. Every challenge passed. Badge glowed steady, brilliant green. He closed the mission file. Typed final words: "Leo and squad cleared. Full allies. Protect at all costs." Then he followed them into the light.

QUESTIONS

<u>Level 10 – The Gut Galaxy</u>

1.   Why are many gut bacteria helpful instead of harmful?

2.   Why do we sometimes crave foods that aren't good for us?

3.   How has Agent T changed from the beginning of the story?

4.   How do your stomach and brain talk to each other?

BALANCE BUILDS STRENGTH
MUSCLE TOWN
IMMUNE CITY
SLEEP SANCT
Defeated Lock Jammer
Beat Lactic Jammer
Beat Lactic Aci Gremlin
BASKET
10

LEVEL 11

THE WAY HOME

King Probiotic bowed, his sauerkraut crown tilting. "The Blood-Brain Express is ready. May your journey home be as balanced as the galaxy you've rescued."

A golden pathway appeared, shimmering softly in the sunlight. Gone were the chaotic tunnels and dangerous highways. Just a smooth, glowing road ahead.

Leo glanced at his friends, then at Flo.

"Is this really it?" His voice sounded small.

Flo smiled, her sneakers sparking brightly. "Time to see the results of your choices."

They stepped onto the path, which carried them gently forward. The walls pulsed with the rhythm of a healthy heartbeat.

Thump-thump. Thump-thump.

"It's so much nicer," Nia said.

"This is what it feels like when the body works together," Flo replied.

The Heart

The path widened into the arterial highway. Leo expected mess and noise, but what he saw was calm and order.

Pink arteries glowed softly. Clean and wide. Red blood cells sped past in neat lanes, oxygen bubbles shining. Vitamins rode smoothly, uninterrupted.

Val and several HDL knights appeared on bikes, creating an honor guard.

"Captain," Val greeted Leo. "You did well."

Leo shot them a look. "You cleaned things up."

Val nodded. "You gave us the tools. Three days of good choices has given my team months of easier work. Keep it going."

She sped off, her squad following.

Leo pressed a hand to the artery wall, feeling its warm, steady pulse.

"They need me," he whispered.

"They always have," Flo said.

Muscle Town

The path led through Muscle Town. Factories buzzed with energy. Mitochondria sang as they worked, careful and focused. New young mitochondria rolled out, glowing yellow.

A large banner read: BALANCE BUILDS STRENGTH.

Jamal stopped, staring in awe.

One worker waved. "Hey! The squad is back!"

Others cheered, whistles echoing in the air.

"We're making reinforcements! More power plants for next time!"

Jamal swallowed, emotional. These were the muscles he'd doubted before. The ones he'd called lazy.

"Moving isn't punishment," he said softly. "It's care."

Nia squeezed his shoulder, and they moved on.

Immune City

Next came Immune City's gates. No alarms. Calm and organized.

Mac greeted them at the entrance, vest spotless and relaxed.

"I heard you were coming," he said, offering three medals marked with a microscope and shield. "For outstanding service."

Leo took his medal, feeling its weight.

"We didn't do it alone."

"Nobody does," Mac said, pointing to the plaza. "The whole city - they all wanted to thank you."

Memoria, Tessa, and Benny waited nearby. The Inflammo tower sat quietly, a kiosk marked EMERGENCY USE ONLY.

Memoria gave each of them glowing vials. "Memory back-up, in case you forget why this matters."

Tessa lifted her visor. "You taught us wisdom: when to fight, when to rest."

Benny bounced, grinning. "You fed the probiotics! My antibodies finally get a break!"

Probiotic envoys drifted by. One handed Nia a sealed envelope. "For worry days," he whispered.

Nia's eyes watered. She nodded.

"Balance isn't weakness," she said. "It's strategy."

Mac saluted. "Safe travels."

The Sleep Sanctum

The path dimmed. Silver moths floated around. The air was clean, smelling of fresh rain.

Inside the Sleep Sanctum, conveyor belts moved glowing boxes. Leo read their labels:

Defeated Lock Jammer. Beat Lactic Acid Gremlin. Resisted Toxina. Saved Nia. Leo saved me.

His memories, neatly filed away.

Adeno appeared, clipboard ready. "You did well. Every victory logged. Every lesson saved."

Jamal watched as a box labeled Jamal: Movement = Strength vanished into the archives.

"This all really happened," he breathed.

"Every second," Flo confirmed.

A gentle chime rang. The crew saluted as the kids passed by.

The Blood-Brain Barrier

The path narrowed, ending at a shimmering wall. Guards stood watch.

"Blood-brain barrier," Flo explained. "It protects the brain. Only good things pass."

A guard stepped forward. "ID?"

Leo showed his hand, where each level's stamp glowed: Steady Fuel, Calmer Patrols, Faster Response, Stronger Barriers.

"Approved," the guard said. "Welcome to the Brain Control Center."

They crossed through.

Brain Control Center

Leo's brain became a galaxy of firing neurons. Zap. Zap-zap. All in perfect rhythm. Conversation flowed.

No chaos, flashing lights, or sugar crashes.

Only balance.

A screen appeared, showing:

HEART RATE: 62 BPM
BREATHING: DEEP AND STEADY
IMMUNE SYSTEM: ACTIVE
GUT MICROBIOME: BALANCED
STRESS LEVELS: LOW
MUSCLE RECOVERY: IN PROGRESS

Nia adjusted her glasses. "We did this."

"You did," Flo said.

Another screen showed three kids on a couch, asleep, controllers in hand.

Leo stared. "That's us."

Flo pointed to a portal labeled CONSCIOUSNESS.

Nobody moved.

Goodbye

"Are you coming?" Nia asked.

Flo shook her head, fading. "I can't. I'm part of your knowledge now. But you'll remember me."

"What if we forget?" Leo said.

"You won't." Flo tapped his chest. "Your body remembers. Listen close."

"You'll face Toxina, Anxiety Titan, Pressure Beast again," Flo promised gently. "But now you know how to keep them small. Daily choices. That's real power."

Jamal wiped his eyes. "You keep fighting too."

Flo smiled. "I will."

They hugged her, warmth and light, barely solid.

"Keep going, captain," she whispered.

She stepped back.

"Go now," she said. "Your world's waiting."

Leo looked at Nia and Jamal. They nodded.

They stepped through the portal together.

Waking

Rising through water, weightless.

Darkness faded. Then light. Blinking. Voices.

Leo opened his eyes.

He was on the couch. Morning light spilled in. His neck stiff, his mouth tasted like old chips.

Nia groaned, pushing up her glasses. "What time is it?"

Jamal sat up, controller dropping. "Did we... was that real?"

Leo examined his palm. No stamps, just skin.

But he remembered everything.

"Yeah," he said. "It really happened."

They sat quietly as sunlight filled the room.

The TV displayed: PLAYER 1 HEALTH CRITICAL.

Leo grabbed the controller.

Pressed start.

Then turned the game off.

"Let's get breakfast," he said, standing.

Nia and Jamal followed.

And this time, Leo knew exactly what to eat.

QUESTIONS

<u>Level 11 – The Way Home</u>

1.   Which part of Leo's body improved the most during the adventure?

2.   How are all the body systems connected?

3.   Which character do you relate to most, and why?

Grease
Goblins
Sugary
Cereal
Syrup
Sugar
Slimes
anxiety
whispers
4-4-4-4
RESTORED

LEVEL 12

HOME BASE IRL

Leo's stomach rumbled as sunlight spilled into the quiet kitchen, waking him.

Sunday morning. 7:43 AM. Pancake scent glided through the air.

His mom, humming at the stove, flipped golden pancakes. Plates and forks waited on the table. Maple syrup gleamed on a stack. Bacon sizzled. Orange juice shimmered in a pitcher. A box of sugary cereal brightened the counter.

All the things Leo usually craved.

Nia and Jamal wandered in, drawn by the smell.

But Leo's chest tensed. He pictured the Grease Goblins, the Sugar Slimes, Toxina's sly voice promising comfort.

"Breakfast!" Mom called. "You three must be starving."

They sat. Leo stared at his plate. Pancakes, bacon, juice, syrup.

His hand almost reached for syrup.

Stopped.

He remembered Muscle Town. The mitochondria, glowing when fueled right, crashing after junk.

"Mom?" Leo spoke up. "Can I make eggs too?"

She paused, spatula midway, surprised. "Eggs? That's new."

"Trying something different," Leo answered.

Nia nudged Jamal. They shared a look.

"Me too," said Nia.

"Same," said Jamal.

Mom smiled, puzzled but pleased. "Fridge has eggs."

Leo scrambled eggs, grabbed berries, poured water instead of juice. He took one pancake, not three. He ate half.

Eggs. Berries. Water.

Steady.

When he finished, he felt full without being stuffed or jittery. Just right.

Jamal, halfway through his bacon, looked up. "I'm not even hungry now."

"That's called balance," Nia said, popping a berry from his plate.

Leo's little brother watched, baffled. "Why are you all weird?"

They just smiled.

Mini-Quest Complete: Steady Fuel Buff Activated.

Mid-Morning: The Couch

The couch, TV, and game awaited, so familiar, so easy.

Leo's brother already hogged the corner, controller ready. "Come on! Dungeon time!"

Nia drifted toward the couch. Jamal started to follow.

Leo paused.

He felt it, the pull of the Sedentary Sloth. Just sit. All day. You earned it.

But Muscle Town's repair crews flashed in his mind.

"Twenty minutes of moving first," Leo said.

Jamal gazed longingly at the couch. "Really?"

Leo nodded. "Twenty. Then games."

"I'm in," said Nia.

Jamal groaned but stood.

They shot baskets outside. Walked around the block. Nothing hard.

Leo expected to feel tired, but energy buzzed through him. Heart thumping, fresh air in his lungs.

The couch waited. But now, he didn't need it.

They played for two hours, without guilt.

Movement Quest Complete.

Afternoon: Homework

Homework glare from the kitchen table, math, English, science, history.

Leo started math. The anxiety whispers crept in.

Too much. You'll fail. What if...

He froze, fingers cold.

"Nia!" he called.

She knew at a glance. "Anxiety Titan?"

He nodded.

"Square breathing?"

He nodded again.

Together, they breathed. In for four. Hold. Out. Hold. Hands steadied.

"Better?" Nia asked.

"Yeah."

Timer set. Twenty-five minutes of focused work. Leo tackled the easy problems first, building momentum. Timer dinged, section done.

Five-minute break. Water. Stretch. Quick walk.

Second round, homework mostly done.

Jamal appeared with finished work. "We actually did it."

Nia waved organized notes. "Pomodoro Quest Complete."

Evening: The Choice

Dinner, pizza. Pepperoni, cheese, grease.

Dad set it out. "Dig in."

Jamal raised his hand. "Can we get salad too?"

Dad blinked. "Did you hit your head?"

"Just want something else," Jamal said.

Mom laughed. "Greens coming up."

They made salad with tomatoes and cucumbers. Ate pizza, one slice each. Then salad, water.

Leo's brother inhaled four slices. "More for me."

Nobody argued. Balance mattered more than being perfect.

One cookie each, slowly, savoring the taste.

Grease Goblins didn't show. Toxina stayed silent.

Dinner Quest Complete.

Night: The Real Test

8 PM. Mike's group text...

Michael:

party tonight!

Finnegan:

Video games

Dylan:

soda, chips till midnight.

Charlie:

Where r u Leo?

Nathan:

Come on!
Don't be lame.

Leo stared at his phone.

Old Leo would have gone, no second thoughts.

He remembered Sleep Sanctum. Repair crews at work while he slept. His brain, muscles, immune system rebuilding.

Would he show up exhausted? Would Anxiety Titan return?

"No,"

Leo typed.

He hesitated.

What if they ditched him? What if...

Flo appeared on the windowsill, a shimmer of light.

She didn't speak. Just waited.

Leo breathed deep.

He sent:

Can't tonight. Maybe next weekend?

Immediate replies.

Nathan:

Ur so boring now

John:

Whatever Leo

London:

K see u in school

Walter sent an emoji.

Chest tight. Anxiety Titan poked at Leo.

Then:
Nia (private chat):

> Not going either. Sleep matters.

Jamal:

> Me neither. Hang tomorrow?

Three together. Different choices.

Not everyone would understand. That was okay.

Flo's whisper (inside or out): "Good choice."

She faded.

The Bridge

9 PM.

Leo left his phone in the living room. Washed up, changed, stretched, breathed. Got in bed with a book.

Lamp off.

"Thanks, repair crew," he whispered in the dark.

Heartbeat slowed. Breathing deep.

His body handled the rest.

Monday Morning

Leo woke up rested, not perfect, but better.

His mind felt brighter. His body steadier.

He made oatmeal, no fuss.

Little brother: "Why?"

"Because it works," Leo answered.

The Bus Stop

Nia and Jamal, already waiting. Silent. Together.

Square breathing, hands in pockets. Cold air. Gray sky.

They felt ready.

Bus doors hissed open. Leo stepped on first. Friends followed.

School

First period, pop quiz.

Leo breathed. Flagged hard questions, tackled the easy. No drama, just strategy.

Lunch, balanced plate. Chicken, veggies, rice, water.

Gym, he tried. Muscles answered.

Walking home, Leo spotted a kid with chips and soda.

Grease Goblins and Sugar Slimes played in the bag.

Leo didn't judge. He just remembered: Gut Galaxy, glowing probiotics, shrinking Toxina.

He smiled, walked on.

The Window

Evening. Leo, doing homework, noticed Flo's shimmer in the glass.

She faded, but left a spark.

Leo waved.

Flo waved back.

Gone, but her energy lingered in every choice, every breath.

Leo was captain. His body a team.

Level 12 Complete.

Achievement: Balance in the Real World.

New Quest: Keep Going.

Flo: Still here. Always.

QUESTIONS

Level 12 – Home Base IRL

1.   How can understanding your body help you choose healthier habits?

2.   What makes healthy habits hard sometimes? How could you handle those challenges?

3.   How can you encourage others without sounding bossy or preachy?

A warm autumn afternoon.
Six weeks after the events.
PRESENTATION
Excellent
62 GPM
BALANCE ACHIEVED
Mac
arteries staying clean, keep it up.

LEVEL 13
EPILOGUE

Six Weeks Later

Autumn leaves turned orange. October slid into November before Leo realized it, except this year he saw it all. He noticed bright leaves because his gut felt healthy and his eyes clearer. He wanted to move in the brisk air, his body craved activity now. Feeling good wasn't an accident anymore. He could trace it back to all those little choices from weeks ago.

Small steps. Every day. Layering up until they became something bigger.

The Report Card

Leo checked his grades on the laptop. B-plus in math. A-minus in English. His focus didn't dip during tests. No panic attacks before quizzes.

His mom smiled, reading over his shoulder. "Leo, these are great."

"Yeah," Leo replied. There was no bragging. Just a new normal. "I used better study strategies."

He didn't explain: I breathe before tests. I eat real food. I sleep.

But Mom saw it anyway and ruffled his hair. "I'm proud of you."

The Team

Jamal made the basketball team.

Not because he was suddenly spectacular, but because he showed up, every practice. He rested, ate protein and veggies, and his body had fuel to keep learning.

Coach told him, "You've got good work ethic. Stick with it."

So Jamal did. When he got a cramp, he stretched, drank water, ate a banana. He could picture Muscle Town hard at work, even if he never admitted it.

At lunch one day, Nia asked, "How are your muscles?"

Jamal flexed, serious. "Muscle Town is fully operational."

They all laughed. Nobody else got the joke. That was fine.

The Confidence

Nia gave a class presentation. She didn't spiral. She prepped, ate breakfast, slept well. Her hands didn't even shake.

Her teacher wrote, "Excellent research and delivery. Where did this confidence come from?"

Nia smiled. She knew. She slept. She ate well. Her body worked as a team.

After class, she found the envelope the Probiotic Envoy gave her, OPEN ON WORRY DAYS.

Inside:

You are stronger than you know. Feed yourself well. The answers are already inside you.

She smiled and put it back. She didn't need it today, but was glad it was there.

The Setback

In Week Four, Leo caught a cold, a runny nose, sore throat, and fatigue.

He panicked, thinking, I did everything right. How can I be sick?

Then he remembered: you get sick less, but not never.

His fed-and-rested immune system got him better in three days instead of two weeks. Still, on the couch, he ate crackers, sipped ginger ale, and let routines slide.

Once he felt better, the Chaos Gremlin whispered: See, you failed. You can't keep it up.

Staring at his homework pile, his phone buzzed.

Nia: "You sick?"
Leo: "Yeah. Just getting back to it."
Nia: "Don't push. Rest is part of balance."

Jamal: "Then catch up tomorrow. Not today."

Leo stared at the texts. At his homework.

He closed the laptop. Drank a glass of water. Ate an apple. Went to bed.

Tomorrow, he'd catch up. But not today.

Small steps. Even when it's hard.

The Party

Mike hosted another party. Leo went. Pizza. Soda. Games. Chips. The usual.

But Leo only took one slice of pizza, one soda. He played for an hour. He felt good.

Then he stood up to leave.

"What? We just got started!" Mike said.

Leo shrugged. "I need to sleep."

A few kids laughed. Someone joked he was boring.

Leo didn't argue. He got his coat and waited outside in the cold for his mom. In the window, a shimmer, Flo. She looked healthier than ever, waving with a sandwich in hand.

Leo waved back. Flo vanished.

But he could still feel her in his choices. Every breath, every trade-off for a better self.

His mom pulled up. "You're home early."

Leo nodded. "Pretty good reason."

The Conversation

Next day at school, Leo found Nia and Jamal.

"How was the party?" Nia asked.

"Good. I left early," Leo answered.

Jamal frowned. "That's your favorite thing."

"It still is. I just like sleep more."

Nia grinned. "That's growth."

They lingered as kids hurried to class, a little pod in the Monday rush.

Jamal said quietly, "Ever wonder if it was real?"

Nia shrugged. "Do we have to?"

"No," Leo said. "Because we're different now."

Jamal snickered. "True."

The bell rang. They drifted to class. Leo squeezed the envelope in his bag. The one with golden stamps and proof that something extraordinary happened, even if only he could see it.

Six Weeks In

By week six, habits felt normal, balanced breakfasts, regular movement, focused homework, good sleep.

No big transformations. Just stacked wins.

Leo's little brother asked, "Why are you so different?"

"I'm not," Leo said. "I'm just awake, I think."

That night, Mom's phone buzzed with a video call. Dad's face filled the screen, grainy but grinning. "Two more weeks," he said. "Then I'm home." Jamal's parents and Nia's parents would be back around the same time. The neighborhood was about to feel whole again. Marcus climbed onto Leo's lap to wave at the screen, and for the first time in months, the quiet in the house felt like peace instead of waiting. "Two weeks is 14....days, right? Not bad." Marcus laughed.

The Game

Friday night. Leo, Nia, and Jamal on the couch, controllers in hand. New game, same friends.

Before they started, Leo paused, looking at the room.

"Remember when we used to just zone out here?"

"For hours," Jamal smirked.

"And feel gross," Nia added.

"We're not doing that anymore," Leo said.

"But we're still playing?" Jamal checked.

"Definitely. Just differently."

They played for two hours. Leo stood to get water and shoot hoops.

Nia paused the game. "Coming with."

Jamal tagged along.

They shot baskets, then played some more, then made sandwiches and rested. They stopped at a decent hour. No sugar crash, no midnight exhaustion.

Ready for tomorrow.

The Final Moment

Packing up, Leo glanced at the TV's reflection. Flo, clear as day in the armchair, eating fruit and yogurt, smiled and nodded.

Keep going.

Leo nodded back.

We will.

Flo smiled, then faded. But Leo knew she never really left, she was in his choices, in Nia's calm, in Jamal's confident stride, and in himself, knowing he led the team inside his own body.

The Text

Later, Leo got a text from an unknown number:

Cap. It's Mac. Val's squad says the arteries are staying clean. Keep it up.

Leo smiled. He texted back:

Copy. Pressure Beast: staying small. Squad: staying balanced.

Reply came fast:

> That's what I like to hear. See you in there. Stay sharp.

He set his phone down and closed his eyes.

In the dark, he imagined the whole galaxy inside him. Cells working, his immune system on patrol, and mitochondria humming. His brain organizing memories, and his heart beating steady.

He'd earned this: balance for life.

Achievement unlocked: Balance for Life.
New Quest: Always.

QUESTIONS

<u>Epilogue – Six Weeks Later</u>

1.   What changes stuck for Leo and his friends? Why do some habits last?

2.   Why is it important that the characters still face challenges at the end?

3.   If there were a sequel, what would you want the squad to explore next?

4.   Why is the parents coming home from deployment such a big moment for Leo and his friends?

5.   How did Leo grow while caring for Marcus?

6.   What good things happened for Leo, Nia, and Jamal while they were waiting for their parents to come home?

AUTHOR

Author's Note

Dear Readers, Parents, and Educators,

Thank you for joining Leo, Nia, Jamal, and Flo on their adventure! This book was created to spark curiosity and real conversations about how our bodies work.

Good health isn't about perfection. It's about balance, learning from every experience, and making better choices one step at a time. Mistakes are part of the game.

My hope is that Leo's journey helps families talk openly about healthy living as an exciting adventure. Food fuels us, sleep powers us, movement energizes us.

May this story inspire you to celebrate your body's strengths.

With encouragement,
Dr. Spark

ABOUT THE AUTHOR

Dr. Spark is a community health educator and storyteller who believes that learning and laughter are powerful tools for growth. His stories bring science, imagination, and everyday life together to help children understand how the choices they make shape who they become.

Blending his background in wellness education with a love for storytelling, Dr. Spark writes to inspire curiosity, courage, and balance in young readers. His mission is to help children and families thrive, not just in body, but in mind and spirit.

When he's not writing, Dr. Spark enjoys exploring nature trails, discovering new foods, and finding creative ways to make learning fun.

RESOURCES

The adventures in *Leo and the Game Squad* are inspired by real science about nutrition, health, and stress. While the story is fictional, the lessons are practical and meant to start conversations.

Here are trusted resources for further exploration:

- **CDC Kids' Health** – cdc.gov/healthyschools

- **ChooseMyPlate (USDA)** – choosemyplate.gov

- **American Heart Association – Kids** – heart.org/kids

- **Nemours KidsHealth** – kidshealth.org

Important Note: This book is for educational purposes only. It is **not medical advice**. Always consult a healthcare professional for personal medical guidance.

APPRECIATION

This book exists because of the support and encouragement of many wonderful people.

Heartfelt thanks to my wife and family. Your stories and everyday choices inspired Leo, Nia, Jamal, and Flo's adventures. Special gratitude to my son Nathan, whose curiosity and love of pizza sparked the quest to make healthy habits fun.

I'm grateful to educators, health professionals, and community members who champion children everywhere.

Finally, I thank God for the gifts that made this story possible.

With appreciation,
Dr. Spark

NEXT ADVENTURE

Coming Soon: Leo and the Game Squad

The adventure isn't over. It's just about to level up!

Leo, Nia, Jamal, and Flo have discovered the real secret: balance is their greatest superpower. But just when they think they've mastered the game, a new challenge spawns on the horizon.

This time, a villain more sly than Toxina is waiting, one hiding in every home, school, and pocket:

The Screen Time Sorcerer!

Endless scrolling, late-night gaming, and sudden "just one more episode" spells... Can the Squad outsmart the Sorcerer, restore their Balance Bar, and keep teamwork strong, on and offline?

Get ready for the next level in the Leo and the Game Squad series, where the real world and digital worlds collide!

Want to join the quest?

Follow Dr. Spark online for new stories, healthy hacks, and tips.

Send an email with the subject "Updates and Tips" to DrSparkauthor@gmail.com to get sneak peeks, special downloads, and join the adventure mailing list.

Stay tuned Squad, your next mission is about to begin!

REVIEW

Who you'd recommend the book to

A few words about the adventure

On Amazon: Visit the book's page → scroll down to "Write a customer review." Even a short note helps greatly.

Stay Connected with Dr. Spark

Follow Dr. Spark online for more Stories, Health tips, and upcoming Books and Resources:

- DrSparkauthor@gmail.com

- Want updates and to join the adventure, send email with subject: "Updates and Tips"

to DrSparkauthor@gmail.com